Club Room Corpse

A Cassie Hall Mystery

by
Sherry Lodge

For information, email **Cozy Cat Press**, cozycatpress@aol.com or visit our website at: www.cozycatpress.com

COZY CAT
P R E S S

ISBN: 978-1-946063-15-1

Printed in the United States of America

Cover design by Paula Ellenberger
www.paulaellenberger.com

1 2 3 4 5 6 7 8 9 10

Dedicated to all who sleuth

CHAPTER 1

Steal the Look. The headline caught my attention, and I didn't have any residents to attend to, so I picked up the copy of *Runway Magazine* resting on the concierge desk and flipped through the pages featuring killer dresses: A-line, empire waist, and sheath. Each one was so tempting to buy. And the look I wanted: A silk 70s-style print of underwater plants, like coral and green and blue algae, on an A-line frame dress. The A-line cut would fit my curves the best, but I really wished I could pull off the sheath. If only I could nip those problem spots.

Just then, the lights went out! I put my magazine down. Why did the lights always go out during my shift? It was the daytime shift, of course, so it didn't matter as much as it would during the night, but still annoying. And I knew residents were going to complain about it. Any small disturbance was amplified at the Parkstone.

Just then, without anything changing, the lights sprung back on. I went back to my magazine. *Go figure.*

As I flipped through the pages of perfume advertisements and stylish outfit how-tos, something caught my eye. And in a building full of residents who all had high demands, it had all of my attention: A large spread about a New York fashion show in September gracing the back pages. It was only April, but it was never too early to dream. How fun it would be to actually go to a fashion show. I'd never been to a fashion show before, let alone one in New York during fashion week in the West Village. I pictured large purple plumes and tall svelte models with exotic hairstyles all wearing next season's must-haves. That was it. I must go! Maybe Anna Wintour would attend and be at the center of it all, cackling as she flaunted a sharp Armani blazer and sparkling Versace dress. Yes, I had to be there.

Then I stared at the perforated contest entry form. How many people would probably apply? And they were only choosing five winners. But then, I thought about how fun it would be to be in New York. Maybe I could even stop by the Baxter Enterprises headquarters, and check in with my boss, Royce Baxter. I just knew it would all work out perfectly.

I filled out the contest form and stepped away from the concierge desk and walked over to the resident mailboxes, all the while admiring my new Viridian Vine green nail polish. Even after I'd painted them last night, my homicide detective fiancé, Eric, had commented on the eye-catching color instead of looking at the wedding invitation options we had to choose from. And there were plenty.

After a quick trip to the resident mailboxes, I'd get back to the concierge desk. I was nearly at the mail room, when I heard a blood-curdling scream: "He's following me!"

My heartbeat quickened like steps on a treadmill. I shook and almost dropped the contest letter. I looked up to see Mrs. Stella Thornwhistle walking waywardly down the hallway. She was wearing a vertical striped black and white blouse, a black pencil skirt and burgundy kitten heel shoes. They were suede, and I couldn't believe I was coveting the shoes of a woman 40 years older than me. I really needed to go to this fashion show.

Why was she screaming? There wasn't anyone else around.

"Who's following you?" I said, as she hobbled toward me.

She screamed again, "Harold!" She ran straight into the mailroom, but I still didn't see anyone following her. She continued, "Harold, the ghost of my late husband."

"Oh," I said, as if it was all supposed to make sense. "And the ghost was following you?" She caught her breath, and I managed to mail my contest form before I forgot. A fashion week break from the Parkstone was exactly what I needed. Mrs. Thornwhistle reached out for my arm. "He's everywhere."

I took a deep breath. "Mrs. Thornwhistle, I doubt your late husband Harold is haunting the Parkstone."

"Oh, but he is," she said. "He's haunting *me*, and the club room, and the hallways. He's everywhere."

I was hoping this wouldn't be a resident complaint I'd have to relay to my boss, Royce Baxter. And I wasn't sure fending off ghosts fell into the concierge duty categories. "I'm sure it's nothing," I said.

Then the lights flickered. "It's nothing really," I said again, wondering why the lights kept flickering. Then the lights shut off completely.

Mrs. Thornwhistle whispered, "It's Harold."

"It can't be," I said to her consolingly. "Sometimes when there's a storm outside or high winds, the lights go out momentarily."

"Have you looked outside? It's a clear day," she said.

Mrs. Thornwhistle was right. I'd been outside in the courtyard earlier to make my rounds and it was sunny and still. Not a cloud in the sky. It was unfortunate that the lights going out was unexplainable.

Mrs. Thornwhistle's eyes enlarged: "He's after me!"

"Calm down, Mrs. Thornwhistle," I said. "I will be at the concierge desk all day if you need me for anything. And I'll leave a note for Francis, the nighttime concierge. And in the meantime, I think it would be great if you disregarded the notion of a ghost."

"But I can't," she said.

"For your sake," I said. Then I thought about it some more. "For everyone's sake."

Her shoulders slumped. "Well, okay," she said. "But this may be something worth mentioning to Royce. If he thinks it's an electrical problem, it might be good for him to know a ghost is the culprit."

"If the lights keep going out, I'll mention it to Royce," I said.

She smirked. "I'd tell the ghost to leave, but Harold never did listen to me."

"Right," I said, smiling. How was the rest of my day going to go if this is how it started? Mrs. Thornwhistle walked back down the hallway toward the elevators, and I headed back to the concierge desk just in time to catch a delivery man knocking on the lobby doors. Gilbert, the doorman, had stepped away from his post at the doors, and the delivery man was just standing there knocking repetitively. He looked impatient. I wondered how long he'd been there.

I walked over quickly to open the doors. Jet-Setter and Cashmere, the Parkstone cats, slithered out—anything to be outside on a nice, sunny day. The man walked to the delivery truck and then back up the steps, carrying what looked like a bird cage covered with a yellow drape.

"Can you sign for the cage?" he said, holding out a digital signature pad. I hesitated, trying to figure out what exactly he was delivering. "The sooner, the better," he said. "I'd like to get these lovebirds on their way."

"Lovebirds?" I said. "For whom?"

The delivery man handed me a card. "I don't know. All I've got for this delivery is this card and these talkative lovebirds."

I stood there looking at him blankly. The cats had returned. Jet-Setter was in a tizzy racing in circles and Cashmere was purring against my leg looking up at the cage. They sensed trouble. So did I. The Parkstone wasn't expecting lovebirds.

He continued. "If you don't mind?"

"Right," I said, signing the signature pad. He then unveiled the golden cage, which housed two light peach-colored birds with light blue tails that squawked and gnawed at the cage bars.

I was baffled. "Is there an apartment number?"

"No," he said. "Here's the recipient information—or what's left of it."

He handed me a letter that had the top "to address" portion chewed off. I surmised that the damage must have been due to the avian duo The rest of it read: "To the stellar one. May this one be the best. Yours Always."

So cryptic.

Who was *the stellar one*? And who was *yours always*?

The delivery man chuckled. "Those little guys got to the card that was in their cage before I could take it away. So, unfortunately, there's not a name on it and no apartment number." He looked at the card. "And no return address."

I must have looked exasperated because he said, "Not much I can do about that now but say sorry. Looks like you're having a bad day."

Between ghosts and letter-chewing lovebirds, it had been an interesting morning at the Parkstone.

I grabbed the top of the birdcage and it swayed slightly as the lovebirds flapped around. "Bad day," one said. And then the other repeated it. Again and again. There was no way I was going to allow these lovebirds to take up residence in the Parkstone lobby, as cute as they were. We didn't even have anything to feed them. "I'll make sure this delivery gets to whomever it was intended."

"Your guess is as good as mine," he said before hopping back in his delivery truck and speeding away.

Without a recipient name or sender name and nothing else to go on, something told me the Parkstone lobby had just gotten two new feathery inhabitants. I walked back up the steps to the formidable stone building's revolving doors with Jet-Setter and Cashmere in tow and our new feathery additions.

"Bad day," said one. I couldn't have agreed more.

CHAPTER 2

Back at the Parkstone lobby, I filled the bird's feeder dish with bird food, seeds and pellets that I'd borrowed from one of our residents Mary Chris who has two parakeets. Then I added some fresh fruit as well. I read in a book from the Parkstone library that lovebirds enjoy fresh fruit. From the book, I also discovered that they were Peach Face Lovebirds. They really were beautiful. Then I re-filled Jet-Setter and Cashmere's bowls too because they were running in circles around the cage and I didn't want them to feel left out. The Parkstone was feeling like a full—possibly haunted— apartment building.

The lovebirds continued squawking to passersby, who remarkably didn't seem to think they were out of place.

What a day so far.

I sat back behind the concierge desk and decided the lovebirds needed a name. I thought of a few good ones: Flight Risk, Paisley (because I was wearing a gold, green and purple paisley cardigan), Verbatim and Socialite, because they were already befriending the Parkstone residents. Then I thought about what I'd read earlier about the birds being called Peach Face Lovebirds, and I decided to name one Peachy and the other Keen. Peachy Keen—the lovebird duo. Then I thought about the mystery behind the lovebirds, and how we still didn't know for which resident they were supposed to be delivered. I shuddered.

I tucked the card—the only clue—into the concierge desk drawer. I began writing a letter to Royce at the New York headquarters. He wasn't going to believe the turn of events.

Royce,

At the Parkstone today, we received a surprise on our doorstep: two feathery, talkative lovebirds whose favorite phrase is "Bad day," which they repeat to me and all residents who pass by. Since the delivery letter accompanying them had been chewed up by the lovebirds (who I've named Peachy and Keen), we have no way of knowing the intended recipient. For now, the lovebirds reside in the lobby across from the concierge desk. Please let me know if these accommodations are suitable, or if the club room would be more appropriate.

In other news, Mrs. Thornwhistle has been startled by a ghost. I only mention this because the lights *have* been flickering quite frequently lately, and while I don't believe it's from her ghost, I thought it was worth mentioning.

From me, Peachy and Keen, and all the Parkstone residents, we hope all is well in New York.

Cassie Hall

As I faxed the letter, I kept thinking about the fashion show in New York and hoping that would be my ticket to a vacation in September. In the meantime, there was so much work to do: fix everything at the Parkstone, plan Eric's and my wedding, and now take care of a persnickety set of birds.

I began typing a letter to post in the resident portal, asking residents if any of them were anticipating the delivery of lovebirds. If so, they had arrived. And needed a permanent home. Just then, the lovebirds seemed restless, ruffling their feathers, and moving about their cage. The larger one picked at some seeds then fluttered about some more. Then he hopped to the front of the cage and looked up and squawked, "She will remember me."

I stopped typing. It was eerie how humanlike he sounded. He continued. "She will remember me, she will remember me." Who will remember whom? If only he could talk more. I could start solving the mystery of Peachy and Keen.

I finished the resident letter and posted it to the portal. *Hopefully,* I thought, *by tomorrow, someone will have responded, and the lovebirds would be able to live in an apartment, and not across from the concierge desk in the lobby.* Although, the lobby accommodations weren't too shabby. The birds could do lots of people-watching, there were ample seeds, and the ceilings were desirably high on the off chance they were able to sneak out of their cage.

Yes, life was good.

Before my shift ended, I heard a Fax come through from Royce.

Cassie,
Lovebirds?! Why there's no way we can keep lovebirds in the lobby. What a disturbance for residents and guests. I'm sure they're feathery and cute and good companions, but they *must* be kept in the club room, near the courtyard window so they have enough sunlight.
Please do everything you can to track down the intended recipient of the lovebirds. The Parkstone doesn't need another talisman.

But, considering the lights flickering and your ghost scare, maybe it does. Please tell Mrs. Thornwhistle we are looking into the situation with the lights. Most likely an electrical circuit problem. Also, about Mrs. Thornwhistle, please don't forget she has booked the club room for her birthday celebration tomorrow. I know I said to keep Peachy and Keen (good names, Cassie) in the club room. Check with Mrs. Thornwhistle to make sure that's okay with her for tomorrow.
Royce Baxter
Baxter Enterprises

Mrs. Thornwhistle's 75th birthday party! I'd almost forgotten. But how could I forget? She's been talking about it for weeks. Following Royce's orders, I picked up Peachy and Keen's cage and moved them to the club room. I opened the long, green velvet curtains so they could look out over the courtyard. "There you go," I said.

They ruffled their feathers. "There you go."

I got the feeling they didn't like the club room arrangement as much as they did the lobby. And as I was about to walk away, I began to realize that I was going to miss having the squawking lovebirds right across from me. I peered into the cage. "There you go," one said.

"Who mailed you to the Parkstone?"

"Bad day," the other said.

I sighed. As determined as I was to solve this mystery, I'd reached a dead end in my communication with Peachy and Keen. I hated to leave them in the club room, but I had to get back to my concierge desk.

I was closing the door when I heard one squawk, "She will remember me!"

CHAPTER 3

The next morning I checked in on the lovebirds, who seemed in the same good spirits they'd been in the day before. I refilled their water container and provided more seeds. I tried to get them to talk more, but they seemed stuck on the same three phrases from the day before.

Back at the concierge desk an hour later, I had residents to contend with. Mrs. Thornwhistle stood in the lobby.

It was the day of her 75th birthday party, and she prattled on about the clubroom which she believed was haunted by her late husband, Harold. I grabbed my cup of coffee. This could be a while.

Then my eye caught her extravagant earrings—carved jade pineapple-shaped clip-ons with a border made of diamonds and gold. They were even more stunning than the Parkstone's best views.

"It gets deathly cramped in the club room," she said. "I'm worried there won't be enough room for my lengthy guest list—including Harold's ghost."

My job, as concierge, was to allay her fears. But I also had to tell her we needed to add two lovebirds to that list of guests. Some days my tasks were more difficult than others. "How many partygoers are attending?"

"As it is my 75th birthday, I dared invite 75 guests—including the ghost."

"Of course," I said, smiling. The large number was daunting. "The maximum occupancy is 100."

"Marvelous, Cassie! There will be plenty of room," she said smiling, as she adjusted her earrings with nervous excitement. She saw me observing her and said, "They were a gift from Harold, so long ago." She paused. "He said they were one of a kind—like me."

I looked at them closer. They were quite intricate. She continued, her voice much more relaxed than it had been. "They were custom-made in the Orient. In Burma to be exact. Harold was stationed in Myanmar during WW II. Oh, how I worried, and stayed up late at night. I made myself sick thinking about all the bad things that could happen to him. Luckily, he survived and when he returned home, he had these tucked away in his canvas Army bag, just waiting to be tried on by me." She paused. I could see a tear forming. "Oh, I was so thankful he was home. I would've been okay if he'd brought me a lump of coal."

"I was going to ask where I could get a pair," I said, "but it looks like they're so vintage and unique that I wouldn't stand a chance of finding ones quite like them." And I agreed with Harold. Mrs. Thornwhistle was unique.

"Not unless you know a handsome army man stationed in Burma," she said, gently fidgeting with one of the earrings. "They remind me of him, you know."

I didn't know any army men overseas. Just one man here at home, who had stolen my heart and put a ring on my finger. I could relate to Mrs. Thornwhistle being swept up in love though. Life was better with my fiancé, so I understood Mrs. Thornwhistle's desire to have her counterpart back. I was beginning to think that maybe the ghost was a manifestation of her nostalgia.

Then I had to break it to her about the lovebirds, who were presently residing in the club room. "Do you like birds?" I began.

She clapped her hands. "Why yes! I do, very much!" she said. "I go bird watching in the courtyard all the time. Do you know there's a great cardinal that lands on the courtyard bench near the crab apple trees? I've named him Casper, because he disappears all the time."

I was beginning to think Mrs. Thornwhistle was obsessed with ghosts. "The Parkstone has recently been the fortunate recipient of a feathery duo of lovebirds named Peachy and Keen who are stationed in the clubroom. Is it all right with you if we add two more names to the party guest list?"

"Why of course! I can't wait to meet Peachy and Keen," she said. "I just love lovebirds. Isn't that a coincidence? I used to have a pair of lovebirds—Harold and I did—many, many years ago."

I smiled. I was relieved to hear that Peachy and Keen being in the club room wouldn't be a problem for Mrs. Thornwhistle during her party.

"How about you fill out this guest list?" I said, handing Mrs. Thornwhistle the Parkstone's party form. "That way we'll know who's an invited guest, how long the club room is reserved for, and how we can contact you if need be. Meanwhile, I'm going to check in on the club room, and make sure all of the decorations have been set up." I tried to remain optimistic for her sake. She had given residents strict orders to bring all of the baked goods to the club room before the start of the party, so that everything would be set up ahead of time.

Just then, Cashmere leapt from the concierge desk and pawed at my blouse, which featured a jungle print with large animals like gorillas, zebras, and leopards. It was a Ted Baker silk blouse and each time I wore it, the cats, Jet-setter and Cashmere, seemed especially jumpy, always pawing at the print, as if it contained real animals. I loved wearing it to work though, because sometimes I thought the Parkstone was a jungle in and of itself, and we were all its inhabitants operating in its large, delicate ecosystem.

Mrs. Thornwhistle began filling out the guests' names, and I walked to the club room with Jet-Setter and Cashmere in tow. The club room looked glorious! The party company that had come by earlier had really gone all out. There were large sparkly purple, gold and silver balloons tied to chair backs and scattered about. Confetti dotted the mahogany table and tiered plates held desserts that had already been left by resident attendees. A large *happy birthday* banner was scrolled across the window that led out to the Courtyard. Everything looked perfectly suited for a 75th birthday party. Even Jet-Setter and Cashmere, who swatted at the balloon strings, seemed to agree. Even the lovebirds looked happy.

I left the door ajar and walked back with the cats following. Jet-Setter somehow managed to bring a balloon with him, the string loop wrapped around his tail.

"Dear, I can't wait for the party," said Mrs. Thornwhistle upon my return. "Besides the lurking spirit, I just love it in the club room. You know, the club room window is where I saw—" She paused, looking faint before regaining her wits. "Oh, never mind."

I thought about the club room and where it overlooked: the crabapple tree courtyard. *What had she seen?* I wondered. She liked bird watching, so maybe she was referring to the cardinals, blue jays or red robins she was always talking about.

Then Mrs. Thornwhistle eyed Jet-Setter. "*Everyone* is ready to celebrate I see," Mrs. Thornwhistle said, clapping her hands and smiling at Jet-Setter's present. She unwrapped the balloon from his tail and said, "I'll take this back to the club room. I hope they haven't outdone themselves."

Just then, the phone rang. "I'll have to take this Mrs. Thornwhistle, but feel free to walk back to the club room and start your party. I'll direct guests to the club room as they arrive."

Mrs. Thornwhistle took the silver sparkling balloon from Jet-Setter. "And don't forget, there are the building guests, too."

She began to walk down the hallway as I answered the phone and Jet-Setter made an attempt to follow after Mrs. Thornwhistle for the balloon back. Cashmere jumped up on top of the concierge desk and gnawed at the telephone cord.

Mrs. Thornwhistle walked away slowly, saying to herself, "If I keep talking, seventy-five will get here without me."

CHAPTER 4

Half an hour later, I walked by the club room to ensure that Mrs. Thornwhistle liked the party decorations and that everything was set for her to celebrate. The door creaked open. It smelled musty and dust particles shimmered in the sunlight through the drawn curtains.

There was no sign of Mrs. Thornwhistle.

"Mrs. Thornwhistle," I said loudly. No response. I walked in, and found her body beyond the mahogany table, lying in the middle of the club room floor, as unresponsive as the plate of oatmeal cookies on the table next to her. She was wearing a green wool blazer and skirt, and off-white kitten heel shoes. Two things were distinctly missing: her remarkable jade earrings.

I gasped.

Had a robber knocked her unconscious and stolen her precious jewelry? If a robber had entered the building, there's no way they could have come through the lobby. I'd been there the whole time. Did they sneak in through the courtyard entrance?

Maybe Mrs. Thornwhistle wasn't dead, just unconscious. Then I felt her pulse. There was none. Next to her on the floor was a half-eaten, crumbled oatmeal cookie with peanuts in the middle, a gum wrapper, and teal-colored sequins that glittered in the light. Who had ever heard of an oatmeal cookie with peanuts?

I knew Mrs. Thornwhistle had a peanut allergy. She always refused the peanut butter and jelly crescents at the catered Sunday breakfast. But something told me she hadn't even known these cookies contained peanuts until after she'd bitten into one.

I looked up to see the lovebirds pacing in their cage. Peachy gnawed at the cage bars and then squawked: "Bad day. Bad day. She will remember me."

His comments gave me the chills. Jet-Setter walked over and purred against my leg then swatted at my jungle print blouse. It was confirmed: The Parkstone was lush with amenities, luxury comforts, and high rollers, but the jungle was fierce, and Mrs. Thornwhistle wasn't just unconscious, she was dead.

CHAPTER 5

I ran to the lobby to call 911. I was shaking. I had just been talking with Mrs. Thornwhistle minutes earlier about her earrings, the ghost of her husband, and her birthday party. I couldn't believe she was dead.

I heard knocking on the lobby doors. An elderly couple stood there holding balloons and two wrapped gifts. And to make matters worse, even more guests and residents were starting to show up to her party.

I attended to the guests first. I briefly told them the party had been cancelled due to unforeseen circumstances, which was a dramatic glossing over the truth. Saying anything unsettling would have rocked their world too much, and I couldn't afford anyone else keeling over while I was on the clock.

Then I quickly called 911. I was promised cops would be there within minutes.

I made a copy of the guest list that Mrs. Thornwhistle had provided. It might come in handy when narrowing down the suspects. Then I headed back to the club room to lock the door in case any other invitees showed up. The last thing I wanted was for them to find the guest of honor, Mrs. Thornwhistle, deceased.

Soon, detectives swarmed the lobby and I directed them to the elegant club room, the scene of the crime. They filled the club room and immediately began wrapping the area with yellow caution tape and taking notes on the crime. Party invitees began appearing for the party and the police made a point to question them all.

Then it dawned on me. Someone was missing. Where was Detective Eric Peters, my Maryland homicide detective fiancée? He wasn't on the scene yet. Normally he was a first responder. I hoped everything was okay.

Minutes later, he arrived looking flustered. "Sorry," he said. "I got here as fast as I could." I smiled, relieved to see him. He continued, "We still have some guys on their way. I called for back up."

More coverage at the Parkstone meant the residents would feel more secure, and that made me happy.

"This is quite a perplexing murder case," I said. "We'll need all the help we can get."

"Murder?" he said. "Cassie, who said anything about murder?"

Now I was flustered. "Well, it must be," I said. "Everyone who lives here knows about Mrs. Thornwhistle's peanut allergy."

"Do they?" he said. "Most allergy deaths are accidental."

That was a good point. I was just assuming that most residents knew Mrs. Thornwhistle couldn't eat peanuts. And since the last two deaths at the Parkstone had been murder cases, I assumed this one was, too.

There had already been two murders at the Parkstone since I'd been concierge. I was afraid a third would put residents over the edge. I glanced around the lobby at the assembled guests.

There was Lydia Kemper, a 70-year-old friend of Stella's, who had just seen her that morning. And Ed Halpern, husband of Anita Halpern, longtime resident and advertising executive at Glow Watches who paced, noticeably agitated. His wife Anita seemed the calmer one of the two until Mary Chris Farley walked in. She looked as though she'd been strolling past on her way to the gym when she heard the news. Mary Chris looked distraught and was caught stealing glances at Ed, who unabashedly returned her interest.

Anita was fuming. She glared at Ed and shook her head. Then she finally stood up and crossed her arms. I didn't know quite what was going on, but sensed something other than Mrs. Thornwhistle's death was casting a shadow in the jungle.

Ed, who was now glancing out the courtyard window, appeared to be trying to hide his fixation with Mary Chris.

I couldn't wait to find out what was going on. My boyfriend, Detective Eric Peters, was on the scene and ready to interview possible suspects when he asked me, "Cassie, did you see anything suspicious?"

I thought for a moment. I hadn't seen many residents that morning except Mrs. Thornwhistle. She seemed slightly faint at times but that was to be expected with the anticipation of her birthday celebration. "Not that I can think of," I said. Besides the elliptical machine being broken, not much else was off kilter at the Parkstone. Until now.

"Keep me abreast of anything you remember," he said, flipping his notebook shut.

"There is *one* thing," I said, remembering my conversation with Mrs. Thornwhistle. "She did say she saw something in the courtyard, but didn't complete her thought."

"Something suspicious?"

I shrugged. "I don't know, but it was important enough for her to mention."

"Got it," he said. "And if there's anything else, let me know. We're looking at alibis and motives that don't stack up."

I nodded. I wished I had inquired more into Mrs. Thornwhistle's story, but hadn't wanted to detract from her big day. Mrs. Thornwhistle was one to talk and talk, but for whatever reason, it didn't seem like that was a story she wanted to go into. Not like how she could talk about her late husband Harold for hours and hours. The residents who had showed up for Mrs. Thornwhistle's birthday looked antsy, and I decided to make myself useful by heating up apple cider for residents and birthday guests.

Next, Eric interviewed Mrs. Thornwhistle's friend, Mrs. Kemper, who was trembling. They settled into the mahogany armchairs near the courtyard window, which poured a glorious amount of sunlight into the room.

"How well did you know Mrs. Thornwhistle?" he said.

"Why as well as I know myself," she said, patting her wavy gray hair. Mrs. Kemper was the oldest resident at the Parkstone, and had been a close friend of Mrs. Thornwhistle's. "I've been friends with her for twenty some odd years at the Parkstone."

"Did she have any enemies?"

She gasped. "Not that I know of. A kerfuffle here and there with the knitting group, but nothing deadly." She paused. "She was also my bridge partner at bridge night on Wednesdays. She always had a story to tell. Could never say for certain whether it was true or not. Always made for an interesting game."

Just then, it began to rain, and the sky outside turned dark. What had happened to the glorious sun? As the rain poured harder and the sky turned into a slate gray, I wondered if the sudden change in weather pattern could be the ghost of Harold. The wrought iron courtyard door clanged into the gate. It must have been left open. Was the ghost of Harold trying to tell us something?

"Cassie, Cassie," I heard Eric saying, "You're about to drop the apple cider glasses."

I snapped out of it just in time to see that the tray of apple cider glasses I was holding was askew. "Oh, thanks." I had to keep it together, for Mrs. Thornwhistle, and the ghost of Harold who I now was convinced was still watching over her.

"And had she seen anything recently that she found jarring?" he asked. I was relieved to hear him ask that question. My sleuthing had been put to good use.

Mrs. Kemper extended a long knobby finger in his direction. "Yes! She did. She had seen something in the courtyard just the other day. But you know, she never really did say what it is she saw."

Eric fidgeted in his seat. "This is a murder investigation, ma'am."

She sighed. "Well, you're the authority after all, but she never actually said what it was she saw." Then she sat upright to command attention. "Mrs. Thornwhistle was in the club room just this past weekend and said she was looking out into the courtyard for the red robin, and, well, did she get more than she bargained for."

Eric leaned in, "What, exactly?"

"She said she'd witnessed a liaison." She gasped as if she still couldn't believe it herself. "On a bench in the courtyard." She paused, waiting for a reaction, but Eric was stone-faced before saying, "Got it. She witnessed a tryst."

"Stella just couldn't believe her eyes," Mrs. Kemper said. "She was so aghast at what she'd seen, she never did tell me who it was between." The she paused. "And to be honest, I always did take everything she said with a grain of salt. She was the building gossip."

I walked over to hand out apple cider to some more looky-loo residents who had just walked in. If Mrs. Kemper was right, that could be motive. Whomever

Mrs. Thornwhistle had caught might want her dead so word wouldn't get out about their liaison. I glared at Ed, the watch executive who was closer by the minute to becoming the prime suspect. I had seen the way he was ogling Mary Chris, and the fierce nature in which Anita had reacted.

Eric glanced over at me and shook his head. He walked over and whispered in my ear, "Stop eavesdropping."

"I think I know the tryst Mrs. Kemper was referring to," I said.

Then he looked at me dead in the eyes. "It doesn't matter. You're not sleuthing this case." I couldn't help it. Besides the murderer, I was probably the last person to see Mrs. Thornwhistle alive. I had sent her to the club room to check on the party decorations. She was so preoccupied with Harold's ghost that I thought it would do her good to see the party decorations and how many residents had already left birthday desserts for her party. The problem is, we had no way of knowing who left which dessert, unless the detectives fingerprinted the plates. Even then, the culprit could have worn gloves. I was so disgusted that someone could have intentionally killed Mrs. Thornwhistle. I eyed Ed who stood with his wife Anita on the other side of the room. What was *she* thinking?

I decided to make a move to find out, despite Eric's warning. "Apple cider?" I said, as they both declined. Anita even gave me a bitter mean glare. I had planned on questioning them, then Eric pulled me aside.

"What are you doing?" he said. "The detectives haven't even questioned them yet."

"I was just offering them a hot beverage," I said, but Eric saw right through me.

"*Cassie*, I know you better," he said. "You were trying to get information about the case."

"Speaking of which," I said, "I assume the detectives will fingerprint the ceramic oatmeal peanut cookie plate."

"Of course," he said. "Leave the investigating up to the detectives. I promise we'll do a thorough job and catch the killer."

There was something I needed to tell Eric about the case, too: Mrs. Thornwhistle's earrings. I was probably the only person who knew she'd been wearing the earrings this morning, and wasn't wearing them now. The killer must have taken them. "There's something…" I said.

"Not now, all right?" Eric said. "You're not on this case."

I gulped. He was really putting his foot down. "It's just that…"

He put his arms on my shoulders, and the cider in the glasses moved. "I'll let you know what we find when we find it, but I want you to stay far away from this murder."

I nodded. "Got it," I said, feeling that if I couldn't start solving this case with the detectives, I needed some way to delve into it and be useful. "I'll let Royce know there's been another murder at the Parkstone."

He nodded. "And Cassie, no more wedding invitation samples, please. Not while this case is underway."

I'd sent him about a dozen to look at earlier, not to mention the batch of samples I'd sent his way before that. "Not until the murder's solved. I got it," I said, biting my lip at the realization that my wedding plans with Eric were being influenced by a murder. I sighed. That was the life of a concierge sleuth engaged to a homicide detective. Deception and murder were always the priority.

Back at the concierge desk, I penned a letter to Royce, who I knew was going to be upset to hear that another murder has happened at the Parkstone.

> Royce,
> It is with a heavy heart that I write to you about the murder of our dear Mrs. Thornwhistle, who passed away—it is believed—after consuming a peanut oatmeal cookie in the club room this morning. Her peanut allergy was a well-known fact here at the Parkstone, and it is astonishing that someone has such a black heart to bake her deathly cookies. From what the detectives gather, it was a fellow Parkstonian, and detective interrogations are underway.
> Peachy and Keen still reside in the club room, but I believe I will temporarily allow them to inhabit the lobby until things settle.
> On the note of Mrs. Thornwhistle's death, let me know how to proceed regarding reaching out to relatives and handling resident inquiries.
> Cassie Hall

After sending the note to Royce at headquarters, I couldn't stand it anymore. I wanted to be involved in the investigation, and Eric wouldn't hear of it. Then I got the idea: I'd snoop in Mrs. Thornwhistle's apartment before the police made it a crime scene.

I grabbed the large key ring hanging behind the concierge desk, and found the key to Mrs. Thornwhistle's apartment. Jet-Setter and Cashmere scampered behind me. I wasn't sure they were going to help my goal of going in stealth mode. I looked down at my spiked high heel shoes. Neither were those shoes, but I was still going to wear them.

I took the elevator to the sixth floor and carefully opened the door to Mrs. Thornwhistle's apartment. But the thing was, it was already opened. Had she forgotten to lock it? It was quiet and smelled of meringue and looked impeccable. Each painting, each throw, each placemat was intentionally placed. I placed the key in my pocket and wished the sunlight from the balcony window would shine brighter inside the apartment, so I didn't have to conspicuously turn on the lights. But no such luck. I couldn't see a thing. I flipped the lights on as quietly as I could. Jet-Setter and Cashmere crept in quietly, too, as if they knew we were sleuthing. I shut the door behind me and then sidled to the kitchen where plates of meringue were carefully wrapped and a glass carafe of orange juice rested on the counter. Then, I heard a man's voice let out a disgruntled sigh from the other room.

Someone else was in Mrs. Thornwhistle's apartment. Who would invade a deceased woman's home?

CHAPTER 6

I looked at Jet-Setter and Cashmere and myself and realized I had done just that. I'd broken into Mrs. Thornwhistle's apartment. But now was not the time to consider moral dilemmas. Now was the time to gather the fur balls and hide. Just as much as this intruder didn't want to be seen, I didn't want to be seen either.

I either needed to find a place to hide or a way out. I looked at the door. It was too far away for me to make it to there in time. *They really ought to redesign these floor plans.* I scooped up Jet-Setter and Cashmere and crouched behind the kitchen counter. My shoes were not the most comfortable, especially supporting all of my weight hunched over, and I quickly undid the straps and took them off. Ahh, at least my feet were free even though I was trapped in a 9 x 9 foot kitchen. I knew the exact dimensions for the one-bedroom kitchens. And 9 x 9 feet was really small when you're already feeling trapped. Given the luxurious state of the Parkstone, the one-bedroom kitchens were kind of cramped. Then crash! I heard a noise from the other room.

It sounded like it could be a lamp, but I couldn't be sure. Was someone vandalizing Mrs. Thornwhistle's apartment? Then footsteps! I held Jet-Setter and Cashmere closer, and tried to crouch even lower under the kitchen counter.

Then the intruder walked into the living room and past the kitchen. They stopped. *Oh, please don't see me!* Maybe they were looking at the gorgeous meringues? Then the footsteps continued on the hardwood floors toward the door. I looked up to see the figure move quickly to the door. Jet-Setter wriggled loose from my hug, and peered over the counter to see the profile of the figure. It was Mr. Beasley from 309, wearing a knit cap and scarf wrapped high around his neck, partially hiding his face.

What was Mr. Beasley doing in Mrs. Thornwhistle's apartment?

I teetered on my high heel peep toe shoes and peered around the side of the kitchen counter. My balance was wobbly and I was about to retreat, when Mr. Beasley's figure emerged. He was lingering in the living room. Just then, he lunged forward and snatched $20 from Mrs. Thornwhistle's elegant side table.

I couldn't believe my eyes! What was he doing? Stealing money from a dead woman was the lowest of the low. And why would Beasley need money? I know I had promised not to investigate the murder, but I hadn't made any promises about investigating theft. I would find out.

After he left, I scuttled forward on my heels, still crouched in case he was still in the vicinity. Jet-Setter and Cashmere were still pawing at the air and trying to wriggle out of my embrace. Finally, when I had decided Beasley was gone, I stood up, let the fur balls free, and surveyed the apartment. Everything looked intact. The most recent copy of *Bethesda Monthly* rested on the kitchen counter. There was a large collection of bird books in Mrs. Thornwhistle's living room library. There was a beautiful maroon knit cashmere shawl draped over one of the armchairs, and a striped knit blanket resting on the back of her suede green sofa. Next to the sofa was a large basket with spools of yarn and knitting needles. Mrs. Thornwhistle must have been a knitter.

Jet-Setter jumped into the basket and quickly tangled himself up in the yellow and pink spools of yarn. *I can't get caught up in this crime.* I untangled Jet-Setter and picked up Cashmere. The detectives would be here shortly, I was sure of it.

The last thing I needed was for them to find me here. I couldn't risk having Eric thinking I was sticking my nose in where he had told me it didn't belong.

With the fur balls in tow, I slipped out of Mrs. Thornwhistle's apartment and headed back to the concierge desk. As I stepped off the elevator, I realized my suspicions were right. Eric walked directly toward me, flanked by two detectives.

"Cassie, where have you been? I've been looking all over for you."

"I was upstairs getting something from my apartment," I fibbed. So far, our engagement was not getting off to a great start in terms of honesty.

Eric look flustered. "What's Mrs. Thornwhistle's apartment number? And we'll need keys."

"Apartment 503," I said. "I'll grab the key." The key was still in my dress pocket, but I walked to the concierge desk and took the key ring from its hook on the wall and pretended to take the key off of it. I walked back over to the elevators where Eric stood with the other detectives. "Here it is," I said, handing him the key. I had already lied to Eric so much, and I had told myself I wanted to go into our marriage without any secrets. And then I thought about the contest I'd entered. That was another thing I wasn't going to tell him about, unless I won and I got to go to New York. He would probably think it was silly.

"Thanks, Cassie," he said. Then he turned to the detectives, handing them the key. "Go on without me. I'll be up there in a second."

They grunted agreement and headed toward the elevators.

Eric turned back toward me, putting his hands on my shoulders. "Cassie, is everything alright? I know there's been a murder, but I'm worried there's something else going on."

He was on to me. "I'm fine," I said. "Really, I'm okay."

"If it's about those invitations, I can take a look at them and help you decide which one to send out," he said in a soft voice.

"It's not about the invitations," I said. "I can make a decision." I was already keeping so much from him about the investigation. Could I go into a marriage keeping secrets from a lead homicide detective when he was probably going to end up seeing right through me anyway?

He smiled. "Okay, that would be great, because it really doesn't matter to me."

"I'll surprise you," I said, smiling. Maybe he wouldn't see through me as much as I thought he would.

He gently squeezed my hand. Then he laughed. "Cassie, you're not good at surprises. But I like that. No secrets. I'm so happy to be marrying such a gorgeous, honest woman," he said, giving me a kiss.

Now the guilt was really setting in.

I could only agreed with one of the two adjectives he'd used, and only when I was wearing my Dior lipstick and eye shadow. And a designer outfit. "Yes," I said. "No secrets before we're married."

He laughed. "And hopefully, none after either."

He began walking away and turned around to give me a classic Eric side smile grin. "Stay out of trouble until I get back."

How did he not know I was keeping things from him? My right eye twitches when I lie. That should have been his first clue.

CHAPTER 7

After narrowly escaping Mrs. Thornwhistle's apartment without Mr. Beasley seeing me, and evading my fiancé Eric, I headed back to the concierge desk. Peachy and Keen were the first on my list of things to check on.

The lobby was surprisingly quiet. Maybe everyone was in the club room, trying to see what had happened? And poor Peachy and Keen were in the middle of it all.

Cashmere and Jet-Setter followed me across the lobby as I instructed the doorman, Gilbert, to inform birthday party guests that the party was cancelled. And that we did not have any information at this time. Why worry them if we didn't need to? He obliged, and Jet-Setter and Cashmere and I headed back to the front desk. It didn't seem the same without Peachy and Keen squawking.

I decided to go get them from the club room, even though Eric had told me to stay away from the crime scene. Peachy and Keen shouldn't be around all that chaotic mess anyway. With Cashmere and Jet-Setter at my heels, I navigated stealthily through all the residents and detectives in the club room until I made it to their cage. "She will remember me," they both squawked. They were stuck on that again.

Eric walked up beside me. "Can you please take those birds away? Anywhere but here. We're trying to run a murder investigation and they're driving me crazy."

"Yes," I said. "I was just about to take these little guys back to the lobby." And then it dawned on me that Peachy and Keen had witnessed the whole murder. If anyone could be helpful during the murder investigation it would be them. If only they could talk more, they could tell me what they heard or saw from Mrs. Thornwhistle or the murderer. The clue to the mystery could rest with Peachy and Keen. I smiled. I would gladly bring them back to the lobby.

I walked back through the club room, even though I desperately wanted to stay and overhear the detective interrogations. Eric was interviewing Mary Chris Farley, and Detective Williams had his cold stare focused on Ed Halpern. I would have loved to have known what Ed Halpern was saying. He always seemed suspicious to me. Always took too much time checking his mail, or lingered just long enough at the coffee machine to overhear my conversations with residents.

The club room looked so stately, even with a majority of building residents now crowded into it. Then sure enough, the room filled with the loud banter of Mrs. Kemper, who could talk anyone's ear off. It looked like she was still talking with Detective Brown. Eric caught my glance from across the room. He motioned with his arm for me to leave. It looked like Mrs. Kemper was close to finishing up her conversation with Detective Brown. She had promised me she would stop by the concierge desk to discuss Mrs. Thornwhistle's sudden death. I knew Mrs. Thornwhistle well as a resident, but Mrs. Kemper knew her on a more personal level, and I was sure she would have some insight as to who would want to harm dear Mrs. Thornwhistle.

I walked back to the concierge desk with confidence. I was going to solve this case too!

As Jet-Setter and Cashmere raced and slid on the lobby's shiny marble floors, I gave Peachy and Keen more seeds in hopes they'd remember something. The larger of the two paced with giant hops around the cage. He seemed happy enough bouncing around his cage and chewing seeds. And then, just when I was about to give up and walk away, he said, "Wow. Cookies. Wow. Cookies. She will remember me."

Cookies! I hadn't heard him say anything about cookies before. Maybe he'd heard the murderer or Mrs. Thornwhistle mention the peanut oatmeal cookies. I lingered to see if he would say anything more, but he got very silent. Then, he hit a very high-pitched "Wow" for quite a while before reverting to phrases like "Bad day" and "She will remember me."

I headed back to the concierge desk and added 'Wow cookies' to the list of Peachy Keen phrases.

At least that was something. I sat back behind the concierge desk. I wrote down a list of Peachy Keen phrases as evidence so I wouldn't forget. Then I looked at the clock. It was after noon. I thought that the police's morning interrogations must be winding down. Mrs. Kemper would be coming any minute.

CHAPTER 8

Twenty minutes later, Mrs. Kemper arrived wearing a dark denim button-down shirt, eggplant-colored corduroys, suede royal blue loafers and a large, gold floral statement necklace with pink rhinestones and diamonds. She looked dashing as always, with her hair in perfect waves.

"Dear, I must tell you first off, that the detectives aren't very happy with me," she said, looking behind me far off in the distance. "I think they were hoping I'd be able to provide them with more information about Stella. And although she was my bridge partner and friend, I don't know everything that was going on in her life. Quite a strange woman she was."

"What made her strange?"

"Well, for starters, we never knew what was the truth with her and what wasn't," she said. "She was very finicky—with friendships, with men. Just life in general was never straightforward when dealing with Stella."

I offered Mrs. Kemper some tea, and she accepted. I walked over to the coffee station and made her a cup of green tea, which she drank readily. "What a warm, crisp cup of green tea," she said. "Thank you, Cassie. At least some things are civil at the Parkstone."

"Not everything is in order," I said, "But we do our best. Things aren't as out of place as some people think. You know, like Mrs. Thornwhistle always complaining about the ghost of her late husband, Harold."

Mrs. Kemper placed the green tea cup down on the concierge desk with such a thud I thought it might spill. "Her late husband Harold?!"

I wasn't as confident in my response this time, "Yes?" I said, more as a question.

"No," she said, shaking her head. "First of all, who believes in ghosts? No one. And secondly, she never had a late husband, let alone one named Harold."

This was news to me. I gasped in astonishment. How could it be? Mrs. Thornwhistle had spent all morning complaining about the haunted club room and the ghost of her late husband Harold. I never thought *not* to believe her. "What do you mean he doesn't exist? She was fearful of the ghost just this morning."

"I mean, Mrs. Thornwhistle was never married," she said. "She has a son named William who lives in London now, but she was never married. She had him out of wedlock. Not sure she was even ever engaged. Stella was a single mother who raised a smart son, and she would always brag that he's in finance. But she never married," Mrs. Kemper said triumphantly, raising her chin. "Loved her birds, she did. But that woman wouldn't know the truth if it flew into her head."

"This is good information," I said. "Did you mention to the detectives that she's never been married."

"Why would I?" she said. "They didn't say anything about a ghost of her late husband."

That made sense. "So what else about Mrs. Thornwhistle don't we know?" I said, thinking that based on what Mrs. Kemper was saying, most of what we did know was false.

Mrs. Kemper, who had resumed drinking her green tea, said, "She loved birds, knitting, playing bridge and doting on her son. Other than that, whatever you think you might know about her, take with a grain of salt."

She stared into her teacup. "But I do believe she witnessed a tryst in the courtyard that day. Too bad she never did tell me who it was."

That could be a huge clue to the case, and now there was no way of knowing who she saw. "The detectives will find out somehow," I said, staying optimistic about everything except my wedding plans, which seemed fragmented now and not a top priority with my fiancé Eric.

Mrs. Kemper finished her green tea. "I know you solved the last two crimes, Cassie. So don't you worry. If I think of something I missed, I'll let you know. In the meantime, do be safe. I, for one, don't feel comfortable with a murderer among us. I trust you feel the same."

I nodded. "It's unsettling at best."

"Very well, dear," she said. "I'll be going now."

She slipped off the stool she'd been sitting on and walked toward the elevators. I hoped she wouldn't be too mad at herself that she didn't find out who the tryst was between. I know I was mad at myself, but there was no use worrying over it now. I walked toward Peachy Keen's cage as they repeated, "She will remember me."

Who was out to kill Mrs. Thornwhistle? Had she told a lie she couldn't get out of? Had she scorned someone in the past? Just then the smaller bird squawked, "Don't mind if I do."

"What?" I said. This was a new phrase from them.

Then he kept repeating, "Don't mind if I do."

Don't mind if I do? Could that be what Mrs. Thornwhistle said to her killer about the cookies? Then Peachy, who I'd determined was the smaller one, completed the sentence. "Wow. Cookies. Be my guest. Don't mind if I do."

That's it! That must have been the exchange between Mrs. Thornwhistle and her killer. I'd have to tell Eric about this recent development and that the lovebirds were a great asset to the case. I was so enthralled in listening to them repeat the remarks that I was oblivious to everything else in the lobby.

Just then, someone snuck up behind me. Their footsteps were so faint I didn't hear them until someone behind me said, "Cassie, another murder? If only these stone walls could talk."

I turned around to see Mrs. Canterbury standing there in her gray corduroy overalls, an off-white ruffled blouse and brown leather clogs. "Do we ever get a break from the sinister, or will the murders at the Parkstone just keep piling up?"

Unfortunately for us, she was right. The murders did seem to be just piling up, quicker than logs in the lobby fireplace. And I didn't know how much more we could handle.

She held a plate of apple pie with ornate acorn and leaf lattice. Mrs. Canterbury was always so thoughtful. She brought the pie to the concierge desk and cut a slice for both of us.

"Last time there was a murder at the Parkstone, I brought you blueberry pie. This time, I brought you apple. Let's just hope there's never a need for a pumpkin pie."

Agreed, I thought. "Who in the world would want to harm Mrs. Thornwhistle?"

Mrs. Canterbury lowered her voice. "I don't know, but I do know that she and Mary Chris Farley got into a sort of a spat last Wednesday."

"Do tell," I said, dishing up another spoonful of delicious apple pie.

"I heard them arguing at the elevators," she said. "It really was none of my business, but they were going on and on about something. Something about the courtyard, and what Mrs. Thornwhistle saw."

I gasped. *The tryst*!

Mrs. Canterbury continued, "So maybe this means something to you. Mrs. Thornwhistle was pointing her finger at Mary Chris, who looked livid. I didn't know what all the fuss what about."

I didn't really know either, but Mrs. Canterbury as always had come through with some very important information. I took another bite of the apple pie. "I'll solve this one, too, Mrs. Canterbury. Don't worry," I said, looking at the apple pie. "I'll save the rest of the pie for later."

Just then, Peachy squawked: "Don't mind if I do."

Mrs. Canterbury looked startled. I explained about the lovebirds, the new feathery friends of the Parkstone and how they were harmless.

"They seem like a good addition," she said. "Maybe they can help get things in order around here."

CHAPTER 9

The detectives had moved their interrogations to the lobby, and left the club room wrapped in yellow caution tape. I wondered if the cookies were homemade or store bought. I assumed if they were home made, the detectives would want to search the residents' kitchens, and if they were store bought, they'd want to check their credit card activity. Unless, of course, the killer paid in cash.

There were so many possibilities, and yet none of them sounded feasible. Mrs. Thornwhistle, while maybe not the most transparent of residents, was nothing but lovable. She always wore a smile and a proper knit blazer and pencil skirt, with kitten heels. She always had a story to tell, whether it was about a flighty bird, or the other women her age who had stooped to wearing wigs.

"Cassie," Eric said, snapping me out of my reverie. "Can you bring over an apple cider for Mary Chris. She's under a lot of duress."

"Of course," I said, hopping off the stool to get the glasses of cider from the club room. I didn't want to go back in there, but I made it quick, ducking under the tape. A few detectives still milled around. I would have to search online for those peanut oatmeal cookies. That didn't seem like a likely combination and most likely weren't sold in that many stores. But still, narrowing it down would be difficult.

I heated up the apple cider and left the club room as quickly as possible. Shivers ran up my spine. I found

Eric in the crowd of people and handed an apple cider to Mary Chris, who was wrapped in a knit blanket.

"This is all so sad," she said, dotting her eyes with a tattered Kleenex. "I was upset with her, but I never would have killed her."

Eric eyed her suspiciously. "What were you two arguing about?" Then he looked at me and motioned for me to leave. I couldn't believe it. Why didn't I get to hear any of the detective interrogations? "I'll find you later, Cassie. Promise." Sure.

With that, I took the rest of the apple cider glasses and made my way through the crowd and back to the concierge desk. Eric and I were going to make a great team when we were married. For now, we definitely weren't partners in solving a crime, or anything else for that matter. I wanted to know more about the investigation. What was Mary Chris fighting with Mrs. Thornwhistle about? If it was about the tryst, who had Mary Chris been with? Was it Ed, who was eyeing her in the club room earlier? Mary Chris may not be as laced up as she appeared to be.

Back at the concierge desk, I heard the beeps of the Fax machine. A letter from Royce.

Cassie,

My heart is truly saddened to hear of the passing of such a wonderful resident and human being as Mrs. Thornwhistle. At forty years with the Parkstone, she was one of our longest and most loyal residents. I want you and everyone at the Parkstone to take care of yourselves and each other. It is imperative that we find who committed such a senseless crime to such a keen soul. As much as I encourage the detectives to find who did this, I am pleading with you to stay away from this crime. I fear the culprit is too brazen.

Let the detectives handle the crime-solving and give your full attention to the residents.

My deepest gratitude.

Royce

That made two people who didn't want me investigating the crime. Maybe it was for the better. I flipped on the computer and looked at the sample wedding invitations I had to choose. Some invitations had more calligraphy than others and were embellished with flowers and floral designs. My head felt overwhelmed. I didn't want to look at anymore samples either. How could I think about choosing my wedding invitation when a resident had been murdered? All of a sudden, the samples were the last thing I wanted to look at. I stood up from the desk to go pretend not to overhear conversations whether Eric liked it or not. Then all of a sudden, Keen said: "I've missed you, Stella."

I gasped. His high-pitched squawk echoed in the lobby. I almost stopped breathing I was so in shock. No one else turned around, too preoccupied with their own conversations.

I ran over to the cage. "What?" I said.

"I've missed you Stella," Keen squawked as he hopped around the cage. Peachy followed suit.

Could that have been the killer talking? What was the connection between Mrs. Thornwhistle and these tiny feathery pets? I wrote that down as another Peachy and Keen phrase. Then Mrs. Kemper walked back through the lobby to get a tea, even though I had a hunch she was looking for gossip. It was perfect timing, as I remembered something earlier that I wanted to ask her about.

Mrs. Kemper had just made her tea and settled into one of the velvet plush chairs in the far end of the lobby when I walked up and said, "Mind if I join you?"

"Why not at all, dear," she said. "I just needed to get out the apartment and be around people with all that's going on."

"I understand," I said. "I got to thinking about our conversation earlier."

"You are such a doll," she said. "Thank you for talking, I really did feel better after having gotten all of that off my chest about Stella. Still feel a pang of guilt that I don't know more."

"Well, that's just it," I said. "You might."

She turned her head to the side. "How's that?"

"Well, you said Mrs. Thornwhistle was never married, so I'm wondering, where did she get such dazzling jade earrings?"

Mrs. Kemper wrapped her hands around her coffee mug. "You mean her pineapple carved jade?"

"Yes, those."

"Gorgeous," she said, "Simply magnificent. And she said she got them at a second-hand store here in Bethesda."

I must have looked perplexed. "A Bethesda consignment store?"

"Why yes, dear," she said. "Don't look so confused. There are only two of them in the area. So it must have been one of them. That's what she said at least. And we all know about Stella's word."

I managed a grimace. This was a bit of a let down. I had pictured Mrs. Thornwhistle's life much different from the reality. Now it seemed as though I didn't know what was truly her life.

"Dear, I wish I had a better answer for you. She said the necklace cost a great deal," Mrs. Kemper said, "but I don't know. Although, by the look of the diamonds on those earrings, I bet they cost an arm and a leg, and maybe some stiletto shoes, too."

I tried to hide my dismay that the story Mrs. Thornwhistle had told me wasn't anywhere near the truth. But why would she lie to me? What did it matter where her earrings came from? Or whether she had been married? It all seemed like a lot to make up.

Mrs. Kemper closed her eyes and I feared she was going to fall asleep in the velvet chair. They were quite comfy. Then Eric walked over.

"Cassie," he said, startling Mrs. Kemper awake.

"I need Ed Halpern's apartment number," he said.

"Oh, why?" This sounded good.

"Nothing really," he said. "It's not a lead, just being thorough, seeing as how he was one of the first residents on the scene."

"He and Anita live in 1210," I said. I couldn't help thinking that Eric was definitely keeping something from me. During a murder investigation was a difficult time to try and make a romance work—let alone an engagement. And I was beginning to think that maybe Eric and I wouldn't make it after all.

He put his hands on my shoulders. "Is she all right?" he said, motioning to Mrs. Kemper who was still in slumber in the velvet chair.

"She's fine," I said, "just tuckered out from the mystery swirling around us."

He smiled. "She has the right idea."

"Mind if I stay with you tonight?" he said. "I'm exhausted and I think I'll be here most of the day dealing with this case."

"Of course, that's fine," I said. "How's everything going with the case?"

"It's going fine," he said. "No suspects yet, but I'll let you know what I find. Do you remember anything about the scene that could be relevant?"

"Nope," I said, disregarding the new information I'd just learned about the earrings. "Not that I can remember."

"All right," he said, giving me a kiss on the cheek. "Back to work."

He began walking through the lobby. Just then Keen squawked, "I've missed you, Stella!"

Eric stopped in his tracks. He walked over to the cage. "Cassie, is he talking about Stella Thornwhistle, the victim?"

I hurried over to the cage. "That's what I thought," I said.

"That's what you thought? So he's said this before?"

"Maybe," I said.

"This could be an essential clue to the case," Eric said, peering in the cage.

"I know," I said.

"You should have told me."

"He only said it once," I said. "I thought maybe it was a fluke."

Then Keen squawked, "Bad day. I've missed you Stella."

"He's very repetitive," I said, "but I agree this could be a clue to the crime."

Eric shook his head. "This is amazing. We've got to figure out what this means."

"So, I'm in on the case?" I said.

Eric smiled. "You have your ways." Then he paused. "I guess I can't keep you from this case if you want to be involved in it. I know sleuthing for is like finding a bargain deal on a Louis Vuitton jacket."

"It just doesn't get any better," I said. "I'll start with Peachy and Keen." He smiled and continued walking through the lobby.

I'd already written down all of their phrases, so unless they said anything more, I was ahead of the game on the Peachy Keen data. Then Mrs. Kemper awoke with all of their squawking. She apologized for falling asleep, which I agreed was difficult to do given the noise level of the lobby.

She patted her gray, wavy hair. "I don't know what got into me," she said.

"There's been a lot of commotion with the murder investigation," I said. "You probably just needed a break from all of it."

"Now I think that's a great idea," she said, steadying herself to her feet. Jet-Setter who had snuggled next to her feet, now leapt to the velvet plush chair. He curled up. He had no problem sleeping amidst the busy lobby happenings.

"I'm just so drowsy," she said.

"Would you like a coffee?" I said. "Maybe the caffeine would help?"

"No, that's fine, dear. You're so sweet. I'm just going to go back to my apartment. Hopefully, the craziness will die down soon. Die. Poor word choice."

"Take care, Mrs. Kemper. Let me know if there's anything I can do to help."

She waved her hand as if to say not to worry. That was difficult to do.

CHAPTER 10

Back at the concierge desk, I looked up the contact information for both Bethesda consignment stores: Vintage Vicky's and Charlene's Consignment, neither of which had a log of selling earrings that matched the jade ones I described to them. One store, Vintage Vicky's, didn't even sell earrings and Charlene's Consignment only sold studs, no clip-ons. I was out of luck. It looked as though the story Mrs. Thornwhistle had told of buying the earrings at a local consignment store was fabricated. So what was true? And how was I supposed to find it out?

Hours passed and the detectives still had no suspects or definite cause of death or motive. The lobby looky-loos had retreated to their apartments and most of the detectives had gone back to the station to conduct work on the case. The club room was still a crime scene though and I had to make sure to shoo away residents who still wandered down that way.

The peanut oatmeal cookies had been taken back to the lab at police headquarters for testing, along with Mrs. Thornwhistle's coffee mug and, of course, Mrs. Thornwhistle herself.

Cashmere and Jet-Setter, who weren't used to this type of excitement were a handful. Jet-Setter kept running in circles in the middle of the lobby. And Cashmere, when she wasn't enjoying the warmth from the fireplace, was leaping onto the paisley upholstered curtains, which was quite a feat.

Back at the concierge desk, I'd decided I'd probably done enough sleuthing for one day. All of a sudden, there was a faint knock on the lobby door. I could see the silhouette of a tall man through the glass.

Gilbert, the doorman, was presently at the coffee machine, so I walked through the lobby to answer the door. The figure was of an older gentleman of great stature. *Another party guest,* I thought. He was late to be a party guest though. The party had been scheduled for hours earlier.

Once at the door, I opened it slightly, so as not to let the visitor in all the way. "I'm sorry to tell you, but Mrs. Thornwhistle's party was cancelled."

"Why that's all right," he said. "I didn't come for the party."

At this point I was very confused. Who was this gentleman, and what business did he have at the Parkstone?"

"Then who are you and why are you here?" I said. Jet-Setter and Cashmere gingerly pawed at the gentleman's shoes.

"I'm here to see Stella," he said. "Stella Thornwhistle."

I hated breaking the bad news, but I'd have to tell this gentleman about Stella's murder as it appeared he must be a friend of hers. "I'm very sorry to tell you..." I said.

"It's all right if she doesn't want to see me," he said. "I understand. I just stopped by on the chance that she might want to see me. I knew nothing was definite." He turned to leave as if he was turning away from the building and a new life, and then stopped. "But how did you know? How did you know to tell me about Stella's birthday party?"

I looked at him blankly. My heart stopped. I hadn't known. I'd just assumed he was here for her party.

"Harold?" As in Harold the ghost who haunted Mrs. Thornwhistle? *That* Harold.

He nodded. "Yes, Harold Eager," he said, holding out his hand, "Pleased to meet you...?"

"Cassie Hall," I said. "The Parkstone concierge."

"Cassie Hall," he said. He continued to walk back down the Parkstone steps. Jet-Setter and Cashmere looked up at me in confusion. I couldn't let Harold go. He was a main link to Mrs. Thornwhistle, and this case needed sleuthing. "Harold, you can come in," I said. "I have some bad news, but please, please, do come in."

And then Harold, the real-life ghost, turned around with a big smile on his face and said, "Don't mind if I do."

CHAPTER 11

Harold was wearing jeans with leather loafers, sharp gray socks with red umbrellas, and a tan-colored button down shirt with a darker brown and tan knit sweater over it. He looked comfortable and yet extremely uncomfortable at the same time.

I was still in awe that the real-life Harold existed, and wasn't a figment of Mrs. Thornwhistle's imagination.

Harold walked in eyeing the ornate marble décor of the Parkstone. "This is my first time here," he said. "Quite lovely." Then Peachy squawked, "Wow. Cookies!" and Harold said, "Pretzels and Pringles made it, I see." He walked straight over to the lovebird's cage.

Pretzels and Pringles? Was Harold the one who'd sent the lovebirds to Parkstone? Was Mrs. Thornwhistle the intended recipient? I guess I should have done a better job sleuthing and put two and two together with her love of birds.

Harold had a huge smile on his face. "What did Stella think? Did she love them?" He paused and scratched his head in befuddlement. "Why are the lovebirds in the lobby and not with Stella?"

There was so much to tell Harold, and I didn't want to overwhelm him with Mrs. Thornwhistle's death. "I didn't know the intended recipient of the lovebirds, because they chewed the letter containing the 'to' information. There was no name or apartment number and no return address."

"Why, I never thought of that," he said. "They were a birthday present for Stella."

Keen hopped to the front of the cage and said, "She will remember me."

Harold blushed. "I may have said that a few times. I guess you have to be careful what you say in front of a lovebird. Stella and I used to have lovebirds together named Pringles and Pretzels, because they used to love Pringles chips. That was so long ago, before we split. And she insisted I take them. I thought she would love having lovebirds again."

"So after you two divorced..."

"Dear, we were never married," he said.

My head was spinning. So not everything Mrs. Thornwhistle had said about Harold was true. I appeared she was a serial liar, and now it was going to be my job to sort through the lies and the truths. I feared this was going to be a long conversation to pull out the truth and leave what were figments of her imagination. "How long did you intend on visiting the Parkstone?" I said.

"Well, I had intended on stopping by and making sure Stella had received the birds. Which looks like it didn't happen. And I was hoping to catch up with her. Truth be told, I have a duffle bag packed for a couple of nights in the case she was fancy on seeing me and letting me in for a few nights."

Harold didn't know it, but he could hold some very important information to the crime. "Where did you drive from?"

"Middleburg, Virginia, about an hour away," he said. "Why?"

"I'm going to check with my boss, Royce, and see if we can provide a guest room for you for the night," I said.

"But what about Stella?" he said. "I'm here to see Stella. I want to wish her a happy birthday."

I crossed my arms and looked him straight in the eye. Imparting bad news was always the worst part of being a concierge, when all I wanted was for Parkstone residents and guests to be happy.

"I have some bad news," I said.

He looked frustrated, "Out with it."

"Stella has died," I said. He gasped. I continued. "She was murdered this morning in the club room right before her 75th birthday party."

He grabbed the edge of the bird's cage to steady himself. "Bad day," Keen said.

When Harold finally came around to speaking, he said, "I just don't believe it. Who would do that to my Stella?"

"That's what we're trying to find out," I said. "The detectives and I are working hard to put the puzzle pieces together."

Just then Eric walked over. "Cassie, is everything okay?"

"This is Harold Eager, Mrs. Thornwhistle's..." And I didn't know how to finish the sentence considering he wasn't her late husband as I'd originally thought.

Harold stepped in between us and shook Eric's hand. "Harold Eager, Stella's boyfriend from many years ago."

I turned to Eric. "I'm going to ask Royce about allowing Harold to stay in one of the guest rooms until he feels well enough to drive back to Middleburg. Also, it may be good to interview him, as I believe he would be a good source of information."

"Yes, Mr. Eager," Eric said. "Looks like you could be helpful to us in putting together the pieces of Stella's past. We're having a difficult time deciphering fact from fiction."

"If I can help my Stella, trust me, I'll do it," he said.

"Great," Eric said. "Cassie will get you accommodated, and I'll be ready for questioning with you around dinner time?"

"Maybe we could all have dinner together?" I said, wanting to be sure I was around for the questioning. I wanted to solve this case now more than ever. "My place at 6 p.m."

"You are very kind," Harold said. "I would like that very much."

"Then it's settled," Eric said.

Then there was a long pause, and Harold looked between the bird's cage and us. "May I ask," Harold said, "how did my Stella die?"

There was a long silence before Eric spoke. "A peanut allergy," he said, looking glum.

Harold gasped. Then all of a sudden, he turned whiter than the ornate marble of the lobby. He grasped his heart. "Come again?"

Eric cleared his throat. "I am very sorry to tell you, Stella died from consuming a peanut oatmeal cookie and suffered complications from her peanut allergy."

Harold gasped again.

Eric continued. "I know this is difficult to understand..."

"It's not just difficult," Harold said, turning completely pale. "It's impossible."

CHAPTER 12

The three of us sat at the quiet end of the lobby with the comfortable plush velvet chairs adding to the luxury of the Parkstone even when everything was a mess. The Parkstone: where luxury could kill, and so could fake peanut allergies.

Eric spoke first, "Harold, I don't understand."

After Harold had calmed down and there was life in his cheeks again, he explained very thoroughly: "Stella never had a peanut allergy."

"What?!" I exclaimed. I couldn't believe it. That's one thing about her I was sure was true. Stella Thornwhistle had a peanut allergy, and it was a known fact around the Parkstone.

Harold continued, "Never in her life. She loved her peanut brittle and peanut butter fudge just as much as the next person. And she enjoyed peanut butter and jelly sandwiches for lunch, and sometimes even breakfast."

It didn't make sense. "She always steered clear of the peanut butter and jelly crescents during the Sunday catered breakfast, and her peanut allergy was a well-known fact here at the Parkstone," I said.

Harold smirked. "Another well-known fact: My Stella liked to lie."

"About everything, it seems," I said.

Then Eric chimed in, "Well, if the peanut allergy wasn't the cause of death, our guys at the tox lab will find out what was."

"I can't wait to find out the results," I said.

"We'll know in a day or two," Eric said. "At least for now we can probably rule out the peanut allergy."

"Yes," said Harold. "Well, I'm glad I can be of some help, so far."

"We appreciate it, Harold," I said, "And I just know Mrs. Thornwhistle would have loved the lovebirds."

"Yes, if she had known they were for her," he said. "If only she had known they were for her."

"She did take note of them when she walked through the lobby," I recalled. "She mentioned how much she loved lovebirds, and had had some as pets, and she talked about the Cardinal who would visit her in the courtyard."

Harold seemed to feel better about that statement. Then I thought of his comment, "If she had known they were for her." What if there were two killers out there looking to kill Mrs. Thornwhistle? Since her peanut allergy *was* such a well-known fact, someone could have targeted her with the cookies thinking she would have a deadly allergic reaction to them. But then another killer came in and killed her with something else, which we'd soon find out from the tox reports. I could be wrong, but I thought it was possible we had two murderers on our hands.

I was going to mention that to Eric, but he was busy talking with Harold. I looked over at the concierge desk from where we sat in the far end of the lobby. Jet-Setter was curled up next to the *"Will be back shortly sign,"* and Peachy and Keen seemed content to hop around their cage and pick at seeds. From this perch, nothing at the Parkstone seemed amiss. But the truth was we had an inscrutable outsider spending the night, two killers on the loose, and enough false statements to wrap the 12-story building in lies.

And then there was the immediate dilemma. What to serve Harold and Eric for dinner?

CHAPTER 13

"Harold, you shouldn't have," I said as Harold handed me a half dozen yellow roses.

"They're from the florist shop down the street," he said. "Bethesda really does have everything, doesn't it? Got out for a bit, and thought it was the least I could do, what with you reserving a room here for me and all."

"Royce had no problem with it," I said, recalling Royce's fax. "Said you can stay as long as you want."

I placed the yellow roses in water in a glass vase. "These are lovely." The yellow picked up on the yellow lace in my Draper James Winston shift dress. *Perfect!* And I was grateful for his kind gesture.

Eric, who had been devouring the olives on the appetizer tray, said, "How long did you and Stella know each other."

"Since we were kids," he said, "Some sixty years ago."

"Was she always adverse to telling the truth?" I said, moving the appetizer trays to the living room, as Eric followed eagerly. I hadn't known what to cook for dinner, but Easter was right around the corner, and I had a lot of eggs on hand. I'd already dyed some for fun, and decided to make the rest into deviled eggs. Then I made salmon and roasted potatoes, Eric's favorite, for the main course.

Eric ate the brie and crackers appetizer happily. Harold just couldn't seem to get over Stella's double life. "Some things I know are facts," he said. "For instance, I know Stella was a great knitter. This I know for a fact, because, well, I'm wearing one of the sweaters she knitted, and isn't it just nifty?" He tugged at the top seams. "It's gorgeous, it really is, and she was so diligent with her knitting."

"It's perfectly knit," I said, looking at the rows. I had also broken into her apartment and seen the spools of yarn and needles in a basket in her living room, so I had a hunch about the knitting. Finally, we had a fact about Mrs. Thornwhistle. Now we just needed more information we could validate.

Harold sipped on some apple cider and ate some olives as he reminisced about Stella. "You know, she kept in touch with me during the war. I was stationed in Burma."

As soon as he mentioned Burma, I thought, *the earring!* That had to be true. There's no way Mrs. Thornwhistle would make up something like that. She said Harold had gotten the carved jade pineapple-shaped earrings from a store in Burma.

"There was a small store," Harold said, "a small Burmese store that had a lot of jewelry, mostly jade, and my eye caught these jade carved pineapples, and I knew Stella had to have them. I also knew her ears weren't pierced. Another Stella fact. So the clip-ons were perfect. Carried them in my duffle bag from the platoon all the way home."

Eric smiled. "And when you returned, you proposed, correct?"

Harold sat up straighter and chuckled. "Now *that's* a story."

I clapped my hands. "Before we begin, I'm going to set the table for dinner. There's deviled eggs, and salmon, and roasted potatoes," I said as both Eric and Harold smiled.

"Let's start dinner now," Eric said, "and then continue the interrogation—I mean interview—after?"

I placed all the plates and utensils on the kitchen table. I wasn't used to having guests over, so we were short glasses and a fork, but we made do.

"That works for me," Harold said. "But can't promise I won't talk about Stella; she's all I've been thinking about for 35 years."

I took a seat next to Harold. I couldn't help but ask, "So why now?"

"Well, I'm not getting any younger, for one," he said, placing the napkin on his lap. "This was maybe my last chance to get in touch with her. Secondly, I don't want to die alone, and the thought of Stella dying alone made me feel as gray as a graveyard. Also, I found out through a mutual friend that she was single."

I shook my head. "But something must have prompted you."

He fidgeted in his chair. "May we eat first?" he said. "I think I'll think more clearly after having something to eat."

Eric chimed in. "Of course, Mr. Eager," he said, "Take as much time as you need. Cassie, how long can Mr. Eager stay in these accommodations?"

I nodded and turned to Harold, "Royce said you can stay here through the end of the week."

Harold patted his lips with the napkin. "That's very gracious of him, thank you."

We all devoured the deviled eggs, potatoes and salmon. I couldn't wait to hear what Harold had to say. What had made him reach out to Stella on her 75th birthday?

After dinner, we crowded into my small living room, with Eric and me sitting on the small loveseat sofa, and Harold taking the green and burgundy armchair. I made coffee for everyone which we sipped before Eric broke the silence. "So, you knew it was Stella's 75th birthday, and you wanted to surprise her…"

Harold placed his coffee mug on the table. "It's more like I was the one who was surprised," he said. "Earlier in the year she had sent me a letter." He paused. It looked as though he might cry.

I moved a box of Kleenex onto the table. "Are you okay, Harold?"

Then he started crying. I quickly got a Kleenex for him and looked at Eric. What had we done?

After a couple of minutes had passed, Harold said, "When I came back from the war, I had two items of jewelry in the duffle bag, those carved jade earrings, and a ring."

"She loved the jade earrings," I said. "She went on and on about how much she liked them, and how much they reminded her of you."

Harold continued. "She didn't see the ring in one of my pockets, but I know she snooped and found the jade earrings in the other. Didn't bother me, but what she didn't know is that I was thinking of proposing."

I clapped my hands. "I just know she would have said yes."

"Well, she did eventually," he said, then his voice dropped, "but it wasn't to me."

I gasped. Eric glared at me. It could be true that I was too emotionally attached to the interrogation, and I decided to show my best poker face. "Who did she say yes to?"

"That's the funny thing. I never did learn who. Apparently, he was a respectable fellow, but no one ever did tell me much about him," he said. "When I got back home, she was eating a lot, had gained a lot of weight, and was acting irrational."

I gasped again. "She was pregnant!"

"You sure are sharp, Cassie. She *was* pregnant. And not with my child," he said. "I wasn't who she had chosen to be with, so I ended up moving to Middleburg and getting on with my life until one day out of the blue…what do you know? Stellar Stella is thinking about me, and wrote me a note to prove it. I've got it at home, folded neatly in the cupboard. She says she can't stop thinking about me all these years. That's when I sent her the lovebirds, as a token of my love, and thought I'd see how it went from there. And, well, it didn't go very far, did it?."

"Do you know of anyone who would have wanted to harm Stella?" I said.

"Not a soul. She was such a kind person, to everyone. She always had more friends than I, and was more outgoing. Involved in everything from book clubs, to swing dancing lessons," he said. "I can tell you whoever killed Stella didn't have a good reason."

"That's why we're going to do everything we can to find her killer," I said, approaching the case with new resolve. Why had Stella reached out to Harold at this moment, after all those years?

Harold fidgeted in his chair. "One vice she did have, if I've got to think of one is that the truth was never her friend. And if someone caught her in a lie, I could see that not going well."

"Either way," I said, "we'll find out who did this."

Eric nodded and Harold took another sip of coffee. "If I know Stella, even half as well as I think I did, the road to getting there won't exactly be direct."

I agreed with Harold. And I was prepared to follow every clue to where it would lead.

CHAPTER 14

The next morning, Mrs. Canterbury stopped by the concierge desk to see how the case was progressing and drop off some homemade chocolate chip cookies.

"I guess maybe I should stop making cookies, seeing as how they can be deadly and all," Mrs. Canterbury said, placing the plate on top of the desk. Minutes later, I had to shoo away Jet-Setter and Cashmere who could smell home-baked cookies a mile away. They came sprinting down the lobby corridor and jumped on top of the desk.

I filled up their food bowls to hopefully offset their cookie hunger. "You're too sweet, Mrs. Canterbury," I said.

"It's the least I can do. You've been working double shifts most nights since the news broke, and they still haven't caught the killer."

I stole a cookie off the plate. "What's the gossip around the building?"

"Interactions among Parkstonians are tense," she said. "No one wants to say the wrong thing, so then people end up not speaking at all. Why, the knitters meeting last night was conducted in dead silence. Poor word choice, I guess."

"Was Stella in that group?" I said, finishing off the cookie.

"Why, no, dear," she said. "She actually knitted very, very well. The group is more for beginners." She paused then said, "Come to think of it, there was a rift between Lydia Kemper and Stella, who did stop by the group once to knit. I remember Lydia couldn't get over what a show off Stella was—purling and knitting rows of a gorgeous sweater for her son. "Show off" are Lydia's words, of course. I thought Stella was a peach."

Mrs. Kemper. I thought back to the morning of the murder and how out of sorts she was and extremely tired. She was so tired in fact she'd almost fallen asleep in the plush velvet chairs of the far end of the lobby.

The morning was still early, and I knew Mrs. Kemper would be by for her morning cup of coffee before 9 a.m. She had a routine she stuck to. Now all I needed to find out was if it had included murder.

Mrs. Canterbury left, leaving me the plate of chocolate chip cookies. She headed out, but not before teaching Peachy and Keen how to say *chocolate chip cookies*, which they kept repeating after she had left. I hadn't seen Harold yet that morning, and I wondered how he was spending his time. He must wonder still about Stella and her life at the Parkstone.

Just then, Gilbert opened the revolving door and let a delivery man through. He was carrying a stack of magazines on a dolly. They were the *Bethesda Monthly* glossy magazines that are free for the Parkstone residents. I stacked some near the lobby's courtyard entrance and strew some copies on the tables in both the far and near lobby. I picked up a copy. It was always good to know what was happening about town, such as places and events.

I ate another chocolate chip cookie, as Jet-Setter curled up on the concierge desk, resigned to the fact that the cookies weren't for him. I flipped through the pages of the *Bethesda* glossy, noticing the marriage announcements. Maybe Eric and I could announce our engagement in the *Bethesda Monthly*? There were upcoming events: dances, town halls and rotary club meetings.

The sky looked dreary and I couldn't have been happier that I was indoors, wearing my navy heels, Kate Spade horseshoe print dress, and Tiffany gold horseshoe necklace. I was about to turn the luck at the Parkstone around. Today would be a lucky day, I was sure.

Building rounds were calling me, but I wanted to finish the magazine first. I needed a break from the case and the Parkstone's morbidity. But I had spoken to soon. I flipped the page and there she was staring at me: Stella Thornwhistle! Her bright, shiny, glossy smile shone right back at me. And her eyes were happy.

CHAPTER 15

Why was Mrs. Thornwhistle featured in the *Bethesda Monthly*? Her happy, smiling face was haunting me. I read the story featured on the page. It appeared that she had won first place in a knitting contest hosted by the magazine. The picture was of her wearing her first place entry, a knit sweater with a scene of the Parkstone courtyard and a cardinal bird. That must be why she was always in the club room staring out at the courtyard. That was also the same time she said she saw something she wished she hadn't.

The sweater did look like a top prize winner. Then I flipped the page to find another surprise. The third place winner was Mrs. Kemper! Her picture was just as glossy and shiny, although her smile was more of a reluctant grin.

So there was a rift between Mrs. Thornwhistle and Mrs. Kemper, and now I understood it a little better. Mrs. Thornwhistle was a better knitter, and had won the prize to prove it. Was it a coincidence that she was murdered a few days before publication of the magazine? I didn't think so.

I couldn't wait for Mrs. Kemper to visit the lobby for her morning coffee. I would be sure to have the magazine open and be ready to question her. In the meantime, I packed up all the magazines I'd strewn about the lobby. I figure there was no need to have the surprise of seeing the newly murdered Mrs. Thornwhistle at the unsuspecting fingertips of residents.

Ping! Just then, the elevator door opened. And out walked Harold Eager. I hid the copy of *Bethesda Monthly* behind my back. "Good morning," I said.

"You seem chipper," he said.

"Not really," I said, thinking I was a better liar than I gave myself credit for. "How did you sleep?"

"Like a bat," he said. "Thanks for asking. And now, if I could just get some coffee, I'll be set for the day."

"Right over here," I said, showing him to the coffee machine. "We have a lot of options, from tea to dark roast coffee."

"This is grand," he said. "I see why Stella liked it here so much."

Harold got his coffee and took a seat in one of the velvet plush chairs in the near end of the lobby close to the concierge desk. Peachy and Keen were very talkative, which seemed to be the case when Harold was around. "Chocolate chip cookies," Keen repeated, until Harold stood up and walked over to their cage. Then Peachy piped in, "Wow. She will remember me."

Harold shook his head. "It seems silly now that I thought these little feathery guys were going to win over Stella for me. I guess love sometimes clouds one's judgment."

Yes, I knew that statement to be true. That's the only reason I could explain why Eric and I had dated for 15 years before he proposed. I was in love with him, and nothing was going to tear me away from him, not even more than a decade of dating before an official commitment.

"I think she would have really like the birds," I said. "Knowing her passion for birds. Peachy and Keen are undeniably cute."

"She would have," he said.

Ping! Just then, the elevator door opened again, and out walked Mrs. Kemper. The only thing I could think about was her third place profile in the magazine for the green and blue triangle-pattern knit sweater that she'd made for the contest. I couldn't confront Mrs. Kemper in front of Harold, because I didn't want Harold to worry. But Mrs. Kemper could be the killer, and I might be able solve the crime.

Mrs. Kemper was loud. It's amazing her perfectly styled curly gray hair didn't come undone each time she spoke. "Gloriously dull day outside, isn't it?" she said, making a coffee at the machine. Then she stared at Harold who sat in the velvet plush chairs.

I spoke up first. "Mrs. Kemper. This is Harold. Harold, this is Mrs. Lydia Kemper."

"How do you do?" he said.

"Better now," she said.

Mrs. Kemper was always one to fawn over men. I thought it best to let her know why Harold was here. "Harold is an old friend of Stella's," I said. "He will be visiting the Parkstone for a few days, given the circumstances."

"So maybe she didn't have such bad taste after all," she said.

"Pardon?" Harold said.

Mrs. Kemper was making me nervous. "I think she meant to say it's nice to meet you."

Harold smiled. "Likewise," he said, looking at Mrs. Kemper in a way that indicated interest, but given her personality and his deep connection to Stella, I thought my eyes must be surely be deceiving me.

CHAPTER 16

Mrs. Kemper was chattering louder and faster than I'd ever seen since I'd known her. She went from one topic to the next, seemingly pulling in Harold closer and closer with each comment.

"And did you know we have catered Sunday brunches here at the Parkstone?" she said. "Those are very popular. Stella just loved to go to the brunches before bridge. But she did avoid the peanut butter and jelly crescents due to her peanut allergy."

Harold scoffed. He looked at me and grimaced. Harold, Eric and I were the only people privy to the fact that Stella's peanut allergy was fake. That reminded me that the tox report might come back today. That would help Eric and me find direction with the case. We'd also need to decide on wedding invitations and I was thinking about not bothering him about it and choosing the invitation myself.

Mrs. Kemper finally took a breath to ask, "Am I talking too much? If I am, just stop me."

Harold began to speak and then she said, "How about you? I know Stella was married to a chap who just passed away, poor fellow. But you. Did you ever marry?"

"The chap who just passed away?" Harold said. "Did you know him?"

"Not personally," Mrs. Kemper said. "Only what Stella had told me about him."

Harold leaned in and made a wide gesture with his hands. "And what exactly did Stella tell you about him?"

For the first time, Mrs. Kemper looked a little nervous as if she'd spoken too much. "Not much," she said, meekly.

"Spill it," Harold said.

I breathed deeply. I felt like it was my job to intervene, even though it was anybody's guess which direction the conversation was going.

Mrs. Kemper bit her lip. "Stella, bless her heart…"

Harold cut her off. "I must know."

"She said they were only married for a couple of years. He was a nice fellow from the area."

"Continue," Harold said.

"He was a salesman…"

"For Julianne's Jewelers?" Harold said, shaking his head.

"You know him!" Mrs. Kemper said, seemingly relieved.

I turned to her and said, "Something tells me a trip down memory lane is not what Mr. Eager needs."

Mrs. Kemper brushed me off and continued, "Why yes, that's who she married." She cupped her coffee mug. "It didn't last long, but she was still so smitten with him."

"Why, I'll kill him!" Harold said.

"Good luck with that," Mrs. Kemper said. "He's already dead. That's what Stella had been talking to me about. His funeral."

And all I could think about was Mrs. Thornwhistle murdered. So I interrupted them, "Please, don't talk about killing people or dead people, please. Not while Mrs. Thornwhistle's death is still unsolved."

Harold stood to his feet. "Why, I'm sorry Cassie. I really am. You and the rest of the Parkstonians seem every bit as nice as I thought Stella was. But this is the one time that maybe I can't forgive her. You see, the salesman she married was a friend."

I gasped! Mrs. Thornwhistle had gotten pregnant by and married one of Harold's friends when he returned from the war.

"How she and others kept that from me for years, is quite spectacular. But leave it up to Stella!"

"I agree. That's some sort of trickery," Mrs. Kemper said. "Her kindness was all a façade."

"Can we not tarnish Mrs. Thornwhistle's character?" I said. "It's not appropriate given the circumstances." But I did find it interesting how much Mrs. Kemper disliked Mrs. Thornwhistle. *Did she have another motive?* I wondered.

"I'm just saying the truth," Mrs. Kemper said. "And I think Harold agrees with me."

He nodded, but he looked too sullen to talk.

Mrs. Kemper continued, "Stella said she was only married for a couple of years." She turned to Harold. "If that makes you feel any better." But by the looks of him it didn't. "And she and Timothy had one son."

Harold clasped his hands. "Stella always got what she wanted. Even when she didn't know what that was." He paused and looked toward me. "Cassie, thank you for your hospitality, but I think I will be going tomorrow. I will stay the night, mainly because I didn't sleep well last night and shouldn't be driving if I'm this exhausted. But tomorrow morning I will be leaving first thing."

"I understand," I said. "If there's anything we can do to make your stay here more pleasant, let me know."

"And if the detectives need me for more questioning. I'll also be at their disposal."

Mrs. Kemper made a fuss. "Why on earth would they need to question *you*?"

"Maybe because they thought I was the one who knew Stella the best," he said. "Turns out that's not true. I'm not sure I can be of much help to the detectives anymore."

I wasn't so sure about that. There must be more he knew that might be important to the case. At least he would be around another day in case the detectives had questions. And Mrs. Kemper seemed so suspicious. As suspicious as a 70-year-old in an upscale apartment building could be. But she looked innocent, wearing emerald green velvet pants, an almond colored knit sweater, and patent leather loafer shoes. Then in her hair, she had glorious small hair clips with black ribbon and topaz, sapphire and ruby beads.

"Those are grand hair clips," I said, thinking that maybe I could wear some quartz hair clips for my wedding. "May I ask where you got them?" I thought it might be too invasive if I asked a resident where they shopped, but couldn't help but think how perfect they would be.

She looked unperturbed by the question but then said, "Why, Cassie, I don't go around giving away secrets like that."

"I do apologize," I said. "Just excited for my wedding."

I resolved that if I couldn't find that exact clip, I'd find a pair similar that I could wear for my wedding.

Just then, Mr. Dash Rhodes entered the lobby, walking his Chihuahua, Moola, who was snippy with Jet-Setter and Cashmere as she passed the concierge desk. *Here we go.* The Chihuahua paraded by with her gregarious owner. Mr. Rhodes had just moved in in February and was already the most high maintenance resident here at the Parkstone. The Chihuahua, Moola, was wearing a hot pink knit sweater and plopped herself down next to Mrs. Kemper's heels. She was usually calm except when she was near the cats.

"Cassie, do you mind?" Mr. Rhodes said. "Do you have a treat for Moola so she doesn't bother dear Lydia?"

I stood right up. "Of course," I said, walking to the concierge desk to get a designer doggie treat called Pooch Mooch for Moola. Upon my return, the three residents were already engaged in a lively discussion, with Moola looking from person to person. I handed Mr. Rhodes the treat to give to Moola. I learned it was better not to get directly involved with residents' pets.

Then Harold introduced himself to Mr. Rhodes. "I'm Harold Eager. I used to know Stella Thornwhistle," he said, shaking Mr. Rhodes' hand. "Pleased to meet you."

Mr. Rhodes gasped. "You're not *the* Harold?"

"Oh no. What do you mean?" Harold said.

"*The* Harold. Stella's ghost?"

"Ghost!" Harold said, upset. "Why no, I'm not a ghost. I'm a person."

"And obviously not her late husband," Mr. Rhodes said, handing the treat to Moola, who curled up on the oriental rug happy as could be.

"No, it has been made very clear, we were never married," Harold said.

"Well, you obviously couldn't be her late husband if you're still alive. And now I can't believe her that you're a ghost," Mr. Rhodes said. "You look very much alive." He was decked out in an Armani pullover, an Apple Watch, custom-tailored khaki's and leather Cole Haan loafers. "Well, as long as you're not haunting this place. It's nice to meet you."

Harold gasped. He looked at me wide-eyed. I thought it was a good time to speak up. "Harold will be staying with us a couple of days to help shed some light on Stella's murder."

"I'm leaving tomorrow," Harold said defiantly.

Mr. Rhodes nodded. "Well, that's sounds just grand. Somebody should make some sense out of her murder. I've only lived here a couple of months, and already two murders." He turned to Moola. "I think she senses the unease, too."

Harold still looked flustered. "And why would I be haunting this place?" Harold said. "Can somebody please explain?"

I explained about the unprovoked power outages, and Stella's stubborn belief that Harold was haunting the Parkstone, which I always found somewhat eerie, given that there was a five-decades-old curse placed on the Parkstone in the 60s after the Baxter family's butler had been found murdered. The mystery had never been solved, and some still claim that the Parkstone for that reason was haunted. It seemed like a good reason.

"Good heavens!" Harold said. "I'm not a ghost, I'm not her late husband, and I'm not sure I want anything to do with Stella anymore."

"I'll toast to that," Mrs. Kemper said, holding her coffee mug in the air. "She was quite a piece of work."

Harold joined her in a toast.

Mr. Rhodes seemed uneasy with the tension. "I don't think it's good for Moola to be around all this negativity," he said. "We're going for a walk." Then he looked me straight in the eye. "I hope all this commotion dies down once I'm back." He paused. "Dies down. Poor word choice. Let's go Moola."

After they left, Mrs. Kemper said, "What a nice fellow. Seems too orderly for the Parkstone, but what do I know?"

"At least you know I'm not a ghost," Harold said. "I don't know who's worse—Stella, or that Rhodes fellow."

Just then, my phone vibrated. I got a text message from Eric: *"Tox report is back. Call me."*

I excused myself from Harold and Mrs. Kemper, who seemed perfectly happy to talk between themselves, and made my way back to the concierge desk. Eric had something important to tell me.

CHAPTER 17

I phoned Eric at the station. He sounded flustered.

"I'm so happy to hear from you," he said. "Big news. The tox report is back."

"And?" I said, eagerly awaiting the results.

"And it wasn't the peanuts that caused Mrs. Thornwhistle's death," he said. "As suspected, Harold was right, she never had an allergy to peanuts. But..." he said, and I couldn't wait to hear the rest, "she did die from complications of a sleeping pill overdose."

"What?!" I said, not believing my ears.

"The contents of her stomach contained a half-eaten oatmeal peanut butter cookie and coffee. And her system had a tremendous amount of sleeping liquid. Over the counter, but in copious amounts, it's deadly."

I gasped. Who would do such a thing to Mrs. Thornwhistle. Someone sinister.

"She got her coffee from the lobby coffee machine that morning. The decaf coffee is made on the spot and easy to tamper with," I said. "But the dark and medium roast coffees and teas are individual packets placed into the machines and it would be impossible to slip in sleeping liquid."

"I can't go in depth about this now," he said. "The guys and I are coming over to the Parkstone to continue our investigations. Keep this quiet for now, but the Parkstone will be bustling with interrogations soon."

"I can't wait to talk about this more," I said. "I have a theory."

He chuckled. "I knew you would."

Harold and Mrs. Kemper walked past the concierge desk and said hi to the lovebirds, who had been quiet all morning. When I got off the phone, they mentioned to me that they'd be in the library playing cards if I needed them.

"Great," I said. "I believe the detectives will be here shortly, so I'll let them know if they need to talk to you." I remembered the morning of the murder and how tired Mrs. Kemper was. She was very groggy and nearly fell asleep in the velvet plush chairs. "Just out of curiosity," I said, "I'm taking a poll, and am wondering whether you drink the decaf coffee made on site, or the other coffee machine options?"

"Decaf, always, love," she said. "Caffeine makes my senses jitter, and I don't like it one bit."

"Noted," I said. "Thanks for participating in the poll. The Parkstone thanks you."

"Anytime," she said. Then she turned to Harold. "Now to the library?"

My guess is that Mrs. Kemper had drunk decaf coffee spiked with the murderer's sleeping liquid meant for Stella. And then there was the plate of oatmeal peanut cookies that were left on the table and intended to kill Stella. Everyone at the Parkstone knew of Stella's peanut allergy and were operating under the theory that said food would kill her. That, I believed, was Murderer #Two, who didn't actually succeed in their plan to kill Stella.

Now for the most important question: Did Stella drink the decaf coffee that day or the coffee from the machine? I couldn't remember. And as the lovebirds rattled off sayings like "bad day," and "cookies," I did my best to think. I couldn't with all the noise.

Then it came to me. "She'd had the coffee from the machine packets, because she'd commented on the noise of the machine.

"That's it, Peachy and Keen," I said. "The clue is decaf coffee."

Keen hopped up to the front of the cage, "Coffee. Bad day. Coffee."

Now, who had planted the sleeping liquid, and how?

CHAPTER 18

Eric and a slew of other detectives arrived within thirty minutes. Mr. Rhodes was just getting back from his walk with Moola, and seemed nervous at the sight of the detectives. "Cassie, what's going on?" he said, reaching down to pick up Moola. "Has there been another murder? I told myself if there was one more murder, I was going to move out."

I shook my head. "There hasn't been another murder," I said. "You're safe to keep renting at the Parkstone."

"Great," he said. "Because I really do love the indoor pool." He paused. "And the wine cellar, and the courtyard. Yes, I'll be staying."

"We're happy to hear it," I said. Then I thought I would do some sleuthing. "It seems like you and Mrs. Kemper are getting along well."

"She's a doll," he said. "Not that other people at the Parkstone aren't nice, but she has been by far the most welcoming."

"That's great to hear," I said, thinking that there was more than meets the eye with Mrs. Kemper and Mr. Rhodes. The detectives began to interview residents as they walked by, and I know Eric didn't want me sleuthing, but I had to find out where Mrs. Kemper had gotten the ribbons and beads she was wearing in her hair. I needed information on where she shopped. "I think her style is great."

"Isn't it?" Mr. Rhodes said. "My wife Penelope is jealous of her. Says she wants to age gracefully like

Mrs. Kemper. Sometimes we're such an old married couple I think we're already there." He paused then said, "You know, when Penelope and I moved it, Mrs. Kemper surprised us with a huge gift basket, an assortment of cheese, crackers, cookies and such."

"Oh really?" I said. "Cookies? "Where was that from."

"Well," Mr. Rhodes said. "Funny story, she wouldn't tell us. But then Penelope did some searching and found out it was from Neiman Marcus. High style."

"That's a really nice gift," I said. Now I just had to find out if Neiman Marcus carried the designer oatmeal and peanut cookies placed on the table for Mrs. Thornwhistle's 75th birthday party.

Mr. Rhodes continued, "Such a nice gift. Come to think of it, we never did repay her…"

I spoke up quickly. I didn't want to be rude, but the only thing I wanted to do then was find out if Mrs. Kemper had attempted murder. "I think we're talking too much, and Moola is getting bored," I said. "I better go make sure everything is okay with the detectives."

"Good idea," he said. "And thanks for looking out for Moola. Sometimes I think a Chihuahua can get lost in this grand Parkstone."

I smiled and headed back to the concierge desk. There was sleuthing to do. I sat at the computer and looked up Neiman Marcus. Just then, Eric stopped by my desk. He leaned across it, looking as handsome as ever. I was so happy I was going to be marrying that man. Then he said, "Could you make an announcement to the Parkstonians that the detectives are here, and we'll have questions. So stay put."

"You got it," I said. "And good to see you."

He smiled and leaned over to give me a kiss. "Likewise."

Then Detective Williams grunted from across the lobby, "Detective Peters, do you mind if we get on with the investigation, not with your fiancée?"

"These guys don't let anything past them," he said.

I smiled. I turned on the overhead announcement Bose sound system and said, "Attention all Parkstonians, the detectives have returned to interview residents regarding the murder of Mrs. Stella Thornwhistle. Please do not leave the building until instructed to do so. Thank you for your cooperation with this matter."

"Perfect," Eric said. "I have to ask, did you see Mrs. Thornwhistle at the coffee machine that morning?"

"Yes," I said. "And I remember she had the coffee made by the machine, not the decaf in the pot."

"Meaning?" he said.

"That it would be nearly impossible for someone to tamper with her coffee before it was in her mug."

"Which we have as evidence, by the way," he said. "Do you remember whether she left it in the club room that morning when you two were talking?"

"She must have," I said. "That's the only way someone could have put the sleeping medicine in it. But I don't remember. I can't say for certain."

He crossed his arms. "I'm thinking she left her mug unattended in the club room, and someone slipped the sleeping liquid in when she wasn't suspecting it."

"How did they know it was her mug?" I said.

"Her name is written on it in large gold letters surrounded by birds," Eric said. "Kind of difficult to miss."

"Right," I said. "By the way, Mrs. Kemper was really drowsy that morning. She said she drinks decaf, which means, the decaf coffee was probably spiked with sleeping medicine, too."

"Williams, get the decaf coffee canister," Eric said, pointing to the coffee pot resting on a table across from the concierge desk.

"Evidence?" he grunted back.

"You bet," Eric said.

All of a sudden, I felt really uneasy. "Do you think someone tried to kill Mrs. Kemper, too?" I said, wondering what kind of killer we were dealing with.

"No," he said. "Don't worry. I know you, and right now you're worried. I think someone at first had the thought to spike the decaf, but then thought better of it. They know who they wanted to target but didn't know for sure if she drank decaf, so why not go right for her mug? There was opportunity. And they went for it."

I shuddered. "The club room door was open, too," I said. "I'd left it open for residents to drop off their baked goods for Mrs. Thornwhistle's party. I didn't think of anyone tampering with her coffee."

I looked down. Eric lifted up my face. "Look at me. It's not your fault."

"I should have done a better job of keeping these premises safe," I said.

"How could you anticipate someone sinister wanting access to Mrs. Thornwhistle's coffee mug?" Eric said. "You don't think like a murderer."

I was about to cry. Eric continued, "That's a good thing."

I was beginning to become very upset thinking about someone wanting to harm Mrs. Thornwhistle. I wiped the tears from my eyes. Good thing for water-resistant mascara! It was so unsettling to think about Mrs. Thornwhistle's murder. And I was so upset, I was starting to think I wasn't a good concierge.

Here I was at the luxurious Parkstone building. Marble interior and all the amenities necessary to keep the residents happy. But they weren't secure. And that was my fault. I had unlocked the club room door, and even though Mrs. Thornwhistle had left her coffee mug unattended, she should be allowed to do that without something bad happening.

Tears welled up in my eyes again. "Maybe I'm not cut out for this job."

Eric grabbed both of my hands. "Don't talk like that. The residents love you," he said.

"Because of me," I said, "Mrs. Thornwhistle was murdered."

"Don't you think you're being a little too hard on yourself?" he said, handing me a Kleenex.

"This place is so expansive and beautiful. I don't deserve to work here," I said.

"The Parkstone needs you now," he said.

I was going to take all that hurt and anger I felt about Mrs. Thornwhistle's death and put it into solving the case. There was another killer to find after all. "I think there are two killers," I said. "I've been meaning to tell you. There are two killers."

"I don't understand," he said. "She died from a sleeping pill overdose."

"But there was someone else who thought she had a peanut allergy, which could be a lot of residents at the Parkstone. And that person brought oatmeal peanut cookies to the club room in the hopes she would die of a peanut allergy."

"You're brilliant," he said.

I smiled. I would solve this crime and avenge my concierge role at the Parkstone.

"There's two killers," I said, repeating it.

"Two killers," Keen said. Oh no! What had I done! Now the birds would be shouting my theory to everyone.

"Two killers. She will remember me," he said.

"Now, maybe you have a problem on your hands," Eric said, looking distraught.

I didn't want residents to know or think there were two killers. Hopefully Keen would pick up another phrase sometime soon.

Eric looked at me straight in the eyes. "I know I told you not to sleuth this case, but you're too smart to sit on the sidelines. We need you involved in putting the pieces together," he said, "*and* I agree with you that someone maliciously brought cookies with hidden peanuts in them to the party in an attempt to kill Mrs. Thornwhistle. If we catch whoever did that they could get time for attempted murder."

I nodded. The minute I had a second to spare, I was going to check out the Neiman Marcus website for deadly designer cookies. And Mrs. Kemper might be looking at jail time instead of Mrs. Thornwhistle's ex-flame.

Eric kissed me and smiled. "I'm going to interview residents now. Find me if you need me," he said. "And good luck sleuthing, even though I know you don't need it."

I smiled and was about to check out the Neiman Marcus website when Mrs. Canterbury appeared at the concierge desk. "Cassie, you two are just too cute for words. And you're engaged! Couldn't be sweeter," she said, placing a platter of lemon pound cake with extravagantly detailed icing along the top and sides. Her eyebrows raised. "And talk about sweet. I put my nervous energy toward baking a lemon pound cake." She placed the plates to the side and began cutting it with a large pastry knife. "There's enough for your beau and the other detectives if they'd like."

"I think they're kind of busy now," I said, "But I'll take a slice for Eric."

"Any leads?" she said.

"Not so far," I said, grimacing.

"Well, I did think of something that might be of interest," Mrs. Canterbury said.

I smiled. "Do tell…"

"Well," she said. "I always thought of Mrs. Thornwhistle as an easygoing person. But there is someone who really ruffled her feathers."

"This sounds good," I said.

She continued, "It's that new resident Mr. Rhodes, and his dog Moo Moo."

"Moola," I said.

Mrs. Canterbury smiled, "Yes, that's it." She lowered her voice. "Now I don't know what happened. You're the sleuth. But she had some pretty choice words for him."

"Thanks for the tip, Mrs. Canterbury," I said.

"So have you set a date?" Mrs. Canterbury said with a side smile.

"Not exactly," I said, taking a bite of the cake. It was delicious.

"What does your dress look like?" she said, slicing another piece for Eric.

"I don't exactly know yet," I said, "but there's this great white pillbox hat I'm going to wear." I had found it a couple months ago in the Parkstone's unused and unrenovated cigar lounge.

Mrs. Canterbury looked befuddled. "Have you picked out the wedding invitations?"

That was a good reminder it was on my to-do list. "Haven't exactly gotten around to that yet."

"Cassie," she exclaimed, "Why I'm beginning to think you and your handsome detective friend aren't having a wedding."

"Oh, we are," I said, consoling her between bites of cake. "It's just that we've both been so busy."

"Why that's understandable," she said, "with the murder and all. That threw everything off."

She was right. I still had to find time to get done the things I needed to get done. And if Eric wasn't available to help pick out the wedding invitations, I'd choose them on my own. "When we do set a date," I said, "I'll let you know." Something told me Mrs. Canterbury was going to be on the guest list.

CHAPTER 19

Things in the lobby were beginning to settle down and I was just about to check the Neiman Marcus website for deadly cookies when Mr. Beasly walked in through the lobby's revolving doors.

"Mr. Beasley," I said, before he could make it to the elevators, "I have a question to ask you." I wanted to know what business he had being in Mrs. Thornwhistle's apartment after her murder.

"I really gotta run," he said.

"I'll just be a second," I said, racing around the concierge desk to meet him in the hallway. We were standing in front of Peachy and Keen's cage when I said, "There's been mention that you were spotted inside of Mrs. Thornwhistle's apartment after she was murdered," I said.

"What? What is this, Cassie?" he said. "I don't have to answer any of your questions."

I took one step forward deliberately placing my heel down hard so that it echoed on the floor. "It's either me or the detectives," I said. "Do you want to answer my questions or theirs?"

His face scrunched up and turned red. "I just don't know where you get off asking questions in the first place," he said. "You're the Parkstone concierge, not the Parkstone police."

He was right, but I wasn't going to stop until I found out why he was in Mrs. Thornwhistle's apartment. "Why were you there, and why did you steal from her?" I said. "That's all I want to know."

"Only half of that is true," he said. "I *was* there, but I didn't steal from her. Look, this has gotten blown out of proportion."

I placed my hands on my hips. "Is this a question you can answer or shall I get the detectives?"

"All right, all right," he said, shaking his head. "Yes, I was in Mrs. Thornwhistle apartment. A couple of weeks ago, she said she wanted to knit me a scarf. We were at the Sunday catered brunch, and I was in a good mood. I said, 'Sure, why not.' Well, let me tell you right now, I really wish I hadn't."

"So, you broke in to get your your scarf?"

"Supposedly, the scarf she was knitting for me," he said. "She asked me what my favorite colors were and I said green and blue. And I gave her twenty dollars. I felt bad that she was going through all the trouble. That's the least I could do. But then when I didn't see the scarf, I wanted my money back."

"So you took the twenty dollars from her side table," I said, shaking my head.

"How'd you know it was the side table?" he said.

"Lucky guess," I said with a smirk.

That seemed to make enough sense, and I wondered what had happened to his missing scarf.

"If I explained it to the detectives, I'd never get my money back," he said.

I wasn't sure he deserved it, but didn't know what to do about it now. I didn't want to admit to Eric that I'd been snooping in Mrs. Thornwhistle's apartment right before the detectives marked it as evidence.

He looked impatient. "Can I go now? The concierge has already taken up enough of my time."

"Goodbye, Mr. Beasley," I said. "And just so you know, the detectives are in-house today, investigating the case of Mrs. Thornwhistle's death. I'll be in touch should they need you for questioning."

"Which they won't," he said, shaking his head. "I had nothing to do with her murder. Just a friendly caution to the concierge."

I smiled politely. I didn't want anything else to do with Mr. Beasley. And I wished Mrs. Thornwhistle had never put any time into making him a scarf. With that, I returned to the concierge desk and was about to sit down at the computer when Harold stopped by with a huge smile.

"Why, this is a lot of activity!" he said. "Detectives swarm the Parkstone and residents rely on memory to piece together details of the murder. I'm sure we're going to get the bad guy."

I smiled. "Yes, we are," I said, hoping it would be sooner rather than later. My head was still spinning from my encounter with Mr. Beasley.

He smiled. "Getting the bad guy. I love it when that happens." Then he paused. "I'd like to stay, if that's okay with you and Royce. I just can't bring myself to leave quite yet, knowing what happened to Stella, and that I might be of use to the case."

"I can ask Royce," I said. "I think it will be feasible that you can stay longer in one of the guest rooms. I'm glad you're enjoying staying at the Parkstone even though it's a tumultuous time."

"I've been through worse," he said, leaning on the counter. "You know I even wanted to go back."

"Where?" I said, not following him.

"To Burma," he said. "Where I fought. I came all the way home, just to want to return. I wanted to live in so many different places. And Stella would just smile and nod. And I knew she'd never leave Bethesda, Maryland. Why would she? Why would anyone for that matter?"

I shrugged. "You left," I said.

"I was nursing a broken heart," he said. "I had returned from the war to a woman who no longer fancied me. My move away from Bethesda was more of a retreat from enemy lines."

I chuckled. "If she got in touch with you after all these years, it meant she was still thinking of you. That means something."

He nodded. "I agree. And I'm going to stick around until her killer is found."

"And if you think of anything that can help with the case, let me or one of the detectives know."

"Cassie, I've been wracking my brain trying to think of information. Why she contacted me. Did she know someone wanted to kill her? Did she know she was going to die? I think of all these questions, and I don't have any answers."

"The detectives are here now," I said, "and they're going to do the best they can to track down the killer."

He held onto the concierge desk now with both hands. "I need to sit down," he said. He walked slowly to the far end of the lobby and sat down in one of the velvet plush chairs. It was quiet there, and I hoped he could regain some of his strength. I, on the other hand, was going to sleuth.

I visited the Neiman Marcus website and searched for oatmeal peanut cookies, and there they were! They were called Oatmeal Peanut Surprise Cookies. They were $60 for a tin and looked just like the cookies that were in the club room on the day of Mrs. Thornwhistle's death. Then I searched the Neiman Marcus website for the ribbon and bead hair clips that Mrs. Kemper had been wearing, and sure enough, they were on the site too. They were sold in various colors of ribbons and types of rock beads and cost $32 each. It was confirmed: Mrs. Kemper shopped by Neiman

Marcus, and I was convinced that's where she'd bought the cookies to try and kill Mrs. Thornwhistle.

I couldn't wait to tell Eric. He was going to be impressed with my sleuthing and my correct assumption that we were dealing with two killers. I grabbed my cellphone and placed the *"Will Be Back Shortly,"* sign on the desk when Harold walked over from the other side of the lobby.

"Cassie," he said. "I've remembered something. It's important."

I sighed. The Neiman Marcus and Mrs. Kemper cookie discovery would have to wait.

CHAPTER 20

I swung around to meet Harold in front of the concierge desk near Peachy and Keen's cage. They look agitated. "Two killers," they said. "Two killers."

Harold's hands flew up in the air. "What do they mean, two killers?"

"Disregard the lovebirds for now," I said. "I think they've just been overhearing too much about the case and didn't get the story straight," I said. "I'll get them more seeds." I got the seeds from behind the concierge desk and fed the lovebirds, who quieted down.

"I just don't know how much more of this I can take," Harold said. "This place is a bit nutty."

I nodded and smiled. He'd sort of hit the nail on the head. "So, speaking of the case, Harold, what did you remember?"

"Oh, goodness," he said. "I almost forgot." He paused. "Well, I was thinking about Stella, and her birthday and everything, and I just got to thinking that it's strange she had a birthday party to begin with."

I leaned in. "How so?"

"Well, she never liked birthdays," he said, looking bewildered.

That was strange.

"Why have a party, and why now? In all the years I'd known her, she'd always despised birthday parties. She wouldn't even let me throw her one. Do you see what I'm saying? There's something strange about it."

I nodded. It fit with the crime of Mrs. Kemper's attempted murder. I had a hunch that after losing that knitting competition and with all her built up anger toward Mrs. Thornwhistle, Mrs. Kemper must have convinced Stella to have a birthday party, just so she could leave out a plate of the Neiman Marcus Oatmeal Peanut Cookies in hopes a peanut allergy would kill her nemesis.

"Thank you, Harold," I said. "You have been tremendously helpful."

He nodded. "Well, I might go now," he said. "Not leave the Parkstone *go*, but *go* upstairs to try and clear my head. All of this murder talk has me out of sorts."

"I think that's a great idea," I said. "If you need anything, call down to the concierge desk."

Now I needed to find Mrs. Kemper. I glanced to the far end of the lobby and saw her talking with Eric. I was going to interrupt. "Excuse me," I said, looking at Eric. "A moment, please?"

He whipped around looking serious. "Cassie, please, I'm in the middle of an interrogation."

Then Mrs. Kemper spoke up. "I'll be around," she said. "Go ahead and talk with Cassie."

I eyed her. She better not go very far.

"Eric…" I said.

"Cassie, what are you doing?" he said. "You can't interrupt me during the middle of an interrogation."

"I can if I have more information about who you're interrogating than you do," I said.

He shook his head and said, "What?"

"There are two killers, right?" I said. "And Mrs. Kemper's one of them."

"How do you know that?" he said.

I explained about the Neiman Marcus purchases, the cookies, and the likely attempt at convincing Mrs. Thornwhistle to have a birthday party in the first place.

"Look, we don't have a lot of evidence to go on in this case, Cassie, but that just doesn't seem like enough," he said. "More than one person can shop at Neiman Marcus. And anyone could have convinced Mrs. Thornwhistle to have a birthday party."

"Yes, but I truly believe it was Mrs. Kemper."

"Plus," he said, "the cookies aren't even what killed Mrs. Thornwhistle."

"As if attempted murder against Mrs. Thornwhistle isn't a crime?" I said, pausing. "I know how we can find it out. Study her reaction. *She* doesn't know the cookies weren't what killed Mrs. Thornwhistle, correct?"

"No, no one does except for the detectives and you," he said, looking like he may have regretted his decision to tell me.

"Follow me," I said. We walked over to the far end of the lobby where Mrs. Kemper had been talking with Eric. She had vanished. We went up and knocked on her apartment door. She wasn't there. We checked the library. No sign of her.

"We've lost her," I said.

"Maybe that's because you interrupted us," Eric said. I shot him a glance. Then he said, "Maybe not."

"Where could she be?" Then I thought. Maybe she went back to the scene of the crime. "She's in the club room."

Eric and I raced down the lobby hallways to the club room to see Mrs. Kemper sitting and knitting in the reading seat next to the courtyard window.

"What a tragedy," she said. "Such a nice, talented woman."

I remembered Mrs. Thornwhistle's shiny, smiling face in the *Bethesda Monthly*. I was so upset with Mrs. Kemper I felt like yelling. But I had to keep a cool head. "Yes, tragic that she died of a sleeping pill overdose," I said.

Mrs. Kemper dropped her knitting. "What?!"

"Yes," I said, "Why do you look so surprised?"

Then Eric whispered in my ear, "That's the reaction we wanted."

Mrs. Kemper began stuttering.

I continued. "Did you expect the weapon to be the oatmeal peanut cookies from Neiman Marcus?"

"Why, yes! That's what killed her—that's what everyone thinks!" she said. "What a wicked woman she was. Everything was a web of lies with her—even until the bitter end."

"I know you like to shop at Neiman Marcus," I said. "That's where your hair clips are from, and the cookies. And you hated Mrs. Thornwhistle."

"Why?" she said, so flustered she put down her knitting. "I have no reason to hate the woman."

Eric took a step back. I continued, "I beg to differ. She was better than you at everything."

"Ha!" Mrs. Kemper said. "She'd like to think that."

"What about the Bethesda knitting competition?" I said, eying her. "She got first place while you got third."

Mrs. Kemper lashed out at me. "How do you know that?"

"It's all out there for everyone to see in the *Bethesda Monthly*," I said, remembering the picture of Mrs. Thornwhistle smiling. "You encouraged her to have a birthday party and invite lots of guests."

"Her and her cardinals," Mrs. Kemper said. "Her and her ghost of Harold. Her and the tryst she witnessed in the courtyard." She shook her head. "I don't regret it. Not one bit. It was just all too much, Stella. And I couldn't take it anymore."

Eric turned toward me, "And that's a good enough confession for me." He paused. "Nice work, Cassie."

"Nice nothing," Mrs. Kemper said.

Eric turned to Mrs. Kemper and put handcuffs on her. She got flustered. "You said it yourself that it wasn't the cookies that killed her. I'm not the murderer."

"Mrs. Kemper, you're arrested for the attempted murder of Mrs. Thornwhistle on the day of her 75th birthday party."

"I'm the only reason she had a party to begin with," she said.

I looked at Eric as if to say, "Told you so."

"She's dead, and she's still causing problems for me!" she shouted. "I can't get a break."

I left the club as Mrs. Kemper and Eric walked through the lobby. Harold happened to be walking out of the elevator at the same time and saw Mrs. Kemper in handcuffs.

"Is she the one who killed Stella?"

I walked up to him. "No," I said, "but she tried to."

"Who are these people?" he said. "Where did Stella live? Amongst a bunch of crooks."

I could understand his disappointment. But there was a lot to love about the Parkstone. "There's a catered brunch on Sundays," I said. "It's quite lavish. If you'd like, they've already set up in the tea room. There's decadent chocolate croissants, fresh blueberry muffins, stacks of pancakes and apple tarts. You must enjoy something to eat. Leave the case up to the detectives."

I shuddered. Now I was beginning to sound like Eric. "Oh," I said, "and the brioches are to die for."

"Cassie, is that a good thing to say here at the Parkstone?"

I blushed. Maybe I could have used a better word. But the brioches were quite good.

"So, what I want to know," Harold said, "is who killed Stella."

"She didn't die because of the peanut allergy poisoning," I said, "as originally thought."

Harold motioned with his hands to get on with it. "Right," he said. "I'm no detective, but I could've told you that one."

"And this is top secret information, Harold," I said. "So you have to promise me you won't tell the other residents."

He shook his head. "I promise. The only person I talked to was that Mrs. Kemper and we found out how corrupt she is."

"We think there was something placed in Mrs. Thornwhistle's coffee," I said, whispering.

He gasped. "Oh, Stella! How horrible. She was such a benevolent person. Unless, you were on her bad side, then boy could she really stick it to you."

I smiled. "I was always on her good side, thankfully." But I knew who wasn't: Mr. Rhodes. And I was going to find out why. "I hope you can stay with us a couple more days while we pursue the investigation."

"You bet," Harold said. Then he patted his grumbling stomach. "Now how about those brioches."

"Down the hall on your right," I said, smiling.

Anyone, even Harold Eager could get used to life at the Parkstone.

CHAPTER 21

I went back to the club room kitchen and made apple cider to hand out to residents being interrogated. It was a great way of striking up a conversation to get more information and for eavesdropping.

With a tray full of glasses of fresh, hot apple cider, I headed to the far end of the lobby. The *"Will Be Back Shortly,"* sign was on the concierge desk, and I needed to be mingling with the residents to sleuth. It's the least I could do for Mrs. Thornwhistle.

The first person I saw was Mr. Rhodes and Moola. "Would you like apple cider?" I said.

"That would be lovely," he said. "Sorry, Moola, you can't have any. But here's a treat." He gave the dog a treat and then said, "If I don't give her treats she'll be running all over the place like crazy." He looked around. "And the last thing this place needs is more crazy."

I couldn't have agreed more. I wanted to know why Mrs. Thornwhistle apparently disliked Mr. Rhodes. We watched as the residents were interviewed again. There was Mary Chris Farley and Mr. and Mrs. Halpern. And Ginnie Langford. I was happy Harold was enjoying a fine brunch without having to worry about the case.

"What a tragedy," Mr. Rhodes said, taking a sip of apple cider.

"I know," I said. "Were you two close?"

"Oh no," he said. "Definitely not. I would not call us close."

"What did you think of Mrs. Thornwhistle?" I said, inquisitively.

"I think she was pleasant." Then he paused. "She wasn't actually that pleasant. She was *okay* to be around, for short periods of time. Like 'hi' and 'bye,'" he said.

"So I take it you didn't like her," I said.

"That's so strong of a phrase," he said, "especially considering the murderer hasn't been caught. It was more like I wasn't too keen on her."

"Sources tell me she wasn't too keen on you either," I said.

He stepped back and shuddered, covering Moola's ears. "I'm trying not to scare the pooch," he whispered.

Just then, I saw Jet-Setter and Cashmere sliding along the marble hallway out of the corner of my eye.

Mr. Rhodes shuddered. "Get those frantic fur balls away from Moola."

Jet-Setter and Cashmere ran circles around us and then continued on their way to the interrogation portion of the lobby, where Eric was interviewing Ed and Anita Halpern.

I wanted to wrap it up with Mr. Rhodes and his sidekick Moola, because I felt like there were other, more important investigations going on underway.

"Why did she dislike you?" I said. "Mrs. Thornwhistle liked everyone."

He sighed. "Fine, I'll tell you why she didn't like me." Then he whispered, "It's because of Moola."

"What?" I said. It sounded so trivial. "Why would she dislike you because of Moola?"

He rolled his eyes. "Well, you know those cardinals in the courtyard she was always adding to her bird watching repertoire?"

"Yes," I said.

"Well," he said, "Moola liked chasing them from the courtyard, just as much as Mrs. Thornwhistle liked observing them. Hence, a problem. Mrs. Thornwhistle was always complaining to me about the rude manners of my Moola. It got so bad that I couldn't bring Moola to the courtyard unless I wanted an earful from Mrs. Thornwhistle."

"That explains it," I said. I could see how that would upset Mrs. Thornwhistle. And she was known to speak her mind.

"But I'll tell you who she really didn't like…"

"Do tell," I said, as we spun around to face the detectives and other residents.

"Ed Halpern," he said. "And I think I know why."

CHAPTER 22

As I moved into the "interrogation" far end of the lobby, I sensed a palpable unease. Residents seemed to be looking over their shoulders. Were they worried about other residents' motives? The detectives were jotting down notes. Ed Halpern twisted his hands together. And his wife, Anita, kept a stiff upper chin, as her gaze followed the longing eyes of her husband who was focused on Mary Chris Farley. The Parkstone was full of twists and turns, and I assumed this was the tryst that Mr. Rhodes was suggesting as the reason Mr. Halpern was guilty.

I caught Eric's attention.

"I only have a minute," he said.

"This won't take long," I said. "I was speaking with Mr. Rhodes earlier and he said he believes the tryst Mrs. Thornwhistle witnessed was between Mr. Halpern and Mary Chris Farley."

"What makes him say that?" Eric asked, crossing his arms.

"Because he's also seen them being romantic," I said, "One day when he was walking Moola in the courtyard before he was kicked out of it because of Mrs. Thornwhistle's bird watching."

"Okay," he said. "This place is quite a fiasco. Always." He paused. "But the Halperns both have alibis."

I looked down disappointed. "Airtight?"

"They are both vouching for each other, that they were in their kitchen having breakfast when Mrs. Thornwhistle was murdered."

"But I swear Ed did it," I said. "He had to have been upset that Mrs. Thornwhistle saw him kissing Mary Chris. That could jeopardize his marriage. Everything!" Although by the looks of Mrs. Halpern, she already knew or was catching on.

Eric shook his head. "We also checked their apartment and there's no evidence of the sleeping medicine that we found in Mrs. Thornwhistle's stomach." He paused. "So, I'm sorry to tell you but we've got nothing to go on with them."

"Ask about the tryst," I said.

He looked at me seriously. "What good is that going to do? I don't think it's linked to the murder."

"I know I'm just going on a hunch here, but I believe Ed killed Mrs. Thornwhistle because he didn't want his wife finding out about him and Mary Chris."

"I think it's a stretch," he said. "By the way he looks at her, I assume Anita already knows."

I crossed my arms in frustration. "So I guess that would mean Mrs. Thornwhistle spilling the beans to Anita wouldn't infuriate Ed." I paused. "Can we just see their reactions?"

Eric looked at his notebook. "I did have it on my list of questions. Don't go far."

I milled around the resident group with the tray of glasses of apple cider, which everyone seemed to enjoy.

Then I saw Eric approach the Halperns. I strategically stood near the corner window within earshot.

Eric started first, "I have to ask, because I've been hearing from residents that Mrs. Thornwhistle witnessed a tryst in the courtyard not too long ago."

Ed looked uncomfortable. Eric continued, "And that this tryst occurred between you, Ed, and Mary Chris Farley."

I scanned the room to see if Mary Chris was present, but it looked like she'd already left. I tried to get a read on Anita's expression but she just looked sullen and detached. I didn't sense any anger. Or surprise. Had she already known? Had Mrs. Thornwhistle told her?

Then, in a quiet voice, Anita said, "She told me." She looked up at Ed expecting a response, but instead Ed looked at Eric and said, "I've had enough of your questioning. I don't have to answer any of your questions. I'm no murderer."

With that, Ed stormed out of the lobby and went to the elevators. Anita, blushing from all the attention, walked down the hallway, either to the library or the club room. A part of me wanted to run and console her, but I wanted to follow-up with Eric too and get his thoughts.

After they left, Eric turned to me. "So have you got any other brilliant ideas?"

I shook my head. "Let's not give up now. There's more than meets the eye here. Anita's reaction was almost stoic, not at all what I would expect given the circumstances."

Eric shrugged. "They're both vouching for each other. That they had breakfast together that morning. I can't bring Ed to the station if he has an alibi."

"Stella used that floral mug that has her name on it. So, the theory is that she left that mug on the table in the club room, correct? And when she was away from the club room, talking to me in the lobby, someone spiked it with sleeping medicine?"

"That's one possibility," he said.

"I didn't see anyone else walk through the lobby at that time," I said. I thought about it some more.

"Although they could have walked down the stairs and down the other hallway and gone in the club room that way."

Eric nodded. "We've considered that option. Unfortunately, there are no cameras in the hallways, so unless someone saw something suspicious, we're not going to get a lead on this case that way."

And then something dawned on me. There was a third option. "What if," I said, shuddering as I considered the possibility, "Mrs. Thornwhistle opened her apartment door that morning to someone she knew. And what if, over banter and coffee, that person slipped the sleeping medicine in Mrs. Thornwhistle's mug."

Eric gulped. "That's another option worth considering. We have to think of all possibilities."

"How horrible," I said. "I've known it was someone at the Parkstone, but thinking about it in those terms is so disheartening." I thought about how I had seen Beasley in her apartment. But I doubted it was him. He just didn't have the motive. Who else would Mrs. Thornwhistle open her door to? Probably anyone at the Parkstone.

I thought and thought and had no way of narrowing down the suspects. And I was still trembling at the thought of Mrs. Thornwhistle opening her door to a killer.

Just then Harold walked up.

"Apple cider?" I said.

"No thanks," he said, "I just had a mimosa. And here I appear in flesh and blood, and, Cassie, you look like you've seen a ghost."

CHAPTER 23

After the thought of someone entering Mrs. Thornwhistle's apartment to kill her, I needed a break from sleuthing the case. It was the first time selecting wedding invitations seemed more appealing than nabbing the bad guy. Even so, I couldn't help thinking about the case. The thought crossed my mind that maybe Mrs. Kemper was guilty of placing the sleeping medicine in Mrs. Thornwhistle's mug, too. Although if she believed Mrs. Thornwhistle was allergic to peanuts—which I believe she did—then she wouldn't have bothered with the sleeping medicine.

And what type of person would think to use sleeping medicine as a murder weapon? Someone who has problems sleeping? I could think of only one resident who had problems sleeping on a regular basis, and that was Mrs. Olive. She was so sweet and plump and I couldn't see her doing harm to anyone, but couldn't just discount her potential involvement. Maybe it was someone who traveled a lot and used sleeping medicine to sleep on planes? There were plenty of people in the building who traveled a lot, including the Halperns.

It was all too much to think about. The detectives were still in the lobby interviewing residents, but many residents, like Mr. Rhodes had already gone on their way after being questioned. I decided to take my mind off the case by sorting through the wedding invitation options.

After hours of going through various flowers and polka dot designs and heartfelt sayings for wedding invitations, I settled on an invitation with yellow, red and pink roses and the announcement, which included date and place, which Eric and I still hadn't decided. I fell into a daydream.

I heard the squawking of the lovebirds. I looked out to the far side of the lobby and out to the courtyard. What a beautiful, serene place with the crab apple trees, and lush topiary. Wouldn't it be wonderful to have the wedding in the Parkstone courtyard? How wonderful! I would run it by Eric first and then ask Royce if that would be feasible. A Parkstone wedding!

I looked over at Eric, who was still interviewing residents. I just knew he would think it was a grand idea. With renewed determination, I set out to find Anita, with Jet-Setter and Cashmere in tow.

I found her in the library where she was looking through some fashion portfolios. She was a top hair and makeup executive at GLOW watches, where her husband Ed worked, too.

I walked in and stood in the doorway admiring the beautiful illustrations of GLOW watches she was flipping through.

She looked up from the portfolio. "Work," she said. "It's always about work."

I smirked. *Except when it was about your husband cheating with another resident.*

She continued, "Is something wrong, Cassie? Can't a resident enjoy the library in peace?"

"Yes, of course," I said. I paused and then got up the courage to say, "I really love those illustrations."

"Oh, these," she said, motioning toward the portfolios. "Yes, well these are great, it's just that I've got to decide on one model watch in all of our collections that will represent the GLOW Watches brand at a fashion show in New York in September."

I smiled. She must have meant the fashion show featured in *Runway Magazine*, the contest for which I'd entered for a chance to attend. She continued, "I'm tired of traveling between here and New York, and choosing a model watch we want to showcase; it's enough to drive a lady nuts."

"Well, don't let me keep you from your decisions," I said. "Just wanted to check in and make sure everything was okay."

"I'm just thinking, this watch. Isn't that a lovely combination of everose gold and diamonds?"

I nodded. It was breathtaking. She continued, "But it may not have *the* right look that says *GLOW Watches: More Stylish By The Minute*. And that's what I'm looking for." She paused. "But what does it matter? The fashion show will be a blast. It always is."

Oh, how I hoped I would win a chance to attend. I could see myself in New York shopping at the boutiques, schmoozing with designers and taking in the fashion.

Anita continued, "Now if you don't mind, I don't want to waste my time."

"Of course," I said, scooping up Jet-Setter and Cashmere. "But if you need anything, don't hesitate."

She gave me a fake smile. "Wouldn't dare think of it."

CHAPTER 24

Back at the concierge desk, I thought about other things I needed to catch up on that I'd put on hold as I was trying to solve the murder case. There was my application to the Fashion College's Right Fit program that I hadn't yet filled out, but was still meaning to. Since it was a certificate program in personal shopping, I'd need a recommendation from someone I'd helped pick out outfits for. I made a note to ask Mrs. Canterbury for her recommendation. And I was hoping she would agree. That was definitely on my to-do list. At least I could cross off wedding invitations and venue. I felt so accomplished.

Then Eric stopped by the concierge desk. "We're just about to wrap up the investigation here shortly," he said. "Still no leads. And sorry if I came across as rude, earlier," he said. "It's just that I really don't think Ed is our suspect. That being said, I don't have a guess as to who is."

"Let me take your mind off the murder for one minute," I said, "and tell you the choice of wedding venue: The Parkstone courtyard."

He smiled. "Cassie, you're brilliant. What a wonderful idea."

"I'm so happy you like my idea," I said, overjoyed. "Right here at the Parkstone."

"I couldn't think of a better place," he said.

"Then it's settled. I'll ask Royce about it next time I talk with him. I don't think they've ever had a wedding at the Parkstone." I paused as my mind drifted to something very important I had to tell him that had been weighing on me as I thought about our wedding. "I want to get something off my chest."

He looked serious. "Sure, Cassie. Anything."

I took a deep breath. "I tried to tell you the day of the murder, but there was so much going on in the club room that morning. And it's just that I don't want there to be any secrets between us before we get married."

He nodded. I continued, "In the morning, before Mrs. Thornwhistle was murdered I noticed she was wearing a pair of stunning pineapple-shaped carved jade clip-on earrings." I paused. "And when I found her murdered, the earrings were gone. Someone had stolen her gorgeous clip-on earrings."

"Cassie, I wish you'd told me this before. We've lost ample time not knowing to look for them," Eric said. "I'll let the detectives know. We'll need to search apartments for the clip-on earrings right away."

"I think it's any important clue," I said. "And I hope you understand why I didn't tell you sooner."

Just then, the elevator door opened. Ping! A frantic Anita stepped off the elevator. "Get him!" she shouted.

My heart raced. "What?" I said. "Who?" I had just seen her an hour earlier in the library and she was fine.

She walked up to Eric and said, "I lied. I was covering for him, but I won't do it anymore. Ed must have killed Mrs. Thornwhistle. We weren't together at breakfast that morning. I lied to save my husband, and the guilt is eating me up. I can't sleep. I can't work."

Eric whistled to gather the detectives. Peachy and Keen were fluttering about their cage at warp speed. And Jet-Setter and Cashmere had hopped on top of the concierge desk to see what all the fuss was about. Before I knew it, the detectives were going to the Halperns' apartment, while Anita hung back in the lobby with Eric and me. I brought her a glass of water, but wasn't sure it was much consolation.

I *knew* Ed was a prime suspect in the case, and I was happy we could finally bring some resolution for Mrs. Thornwhistle.

As they brought Ed out through the lobby, he looked at Anita and said, "Why you little…" He paused. "I might have had an affair with Mary Chris, and Mrs. Thornwhistle saw us kissing in the courtyard…I strayed, but I'm not a murderer! You *know* that."

Anita shook her head. "Ed, I can no longer vouch for you. We didn't have breakfast together that morning, and I refuse to falsely continue to be your alibi."

It was so intense. I hugged Cashmere and hoped the yelling would stop. Ed kept yelling to everyone in the lobby that he didn't do it. What was he going to do, confess?

Eric shook his head. "Cassie, I guess you were right."

"I wish I wasn't," I said. Thinking about how much better I felt that I'd told Eric about the earrings. And now maybe they could find where Ed had hidden them and get them back. Then I decided to ask, "Eric, are you sure you're not keeping a secret from me?"

He looked at the other detectives as they took Ed away through the lobby's revolving door. "Look, Cassie, I've got to go down to the station. They need me."

He walked away as Anita walked up to the concierge desk. "Cassie, you're right," she said. For the first time her bouffant hair style looked like it needed more hairspray. "I think I will need your help."

CHAPTER 25

First things first. I needed to reach out to Royce to make sure he knew the murderer had been caught and that everything was going to go back to normal at the Parkstone. Anita, who was now perched on one of the velvet chairs in the near lobby had said she needed my help. And there would be the other residents' fears to allay. And it was only one o'clock in the afternoon. This was life at the Parkstone.

I wrote a quick letter to Royce Baxter:

Royce,
You will be happy to hear that Eric and the other detectives have apprehended the culprit in the murder of Mrs. Thornwhistle, and it's our very own resident Ed Halpern. Despite the shock and dismay from the residents, life is on its way to getting back to normal at the Parkstone.
And also, I did have an inquiry. As Eric and I plan our wedding, I was wondering if we would have your blessing to hold the ceremony at the Parkstone? We have not yet set a date, but believe, if we have your okay, that we have found the perfect venue. The culprits and murders aside, the Parkstone is quite picturesque.
Cassie

Anita looked so sullen. I brought her a guest present from behind the concierge desk. It was a small box of truffles wrapped in beautiful topiary print wrapping paper.

"A gift to hopefully take your mind off the unrest of Ed's actions," I said.

"Dear," she said, with a strained smile. "You shouldn't have. I need your help if now is a good time."

"I'm all yours," I said.

"Great," she said, heaving a large portfolio on top of my lap. "If you could help pick out a watch, because I haven't the right mind to make a decision, and let me know your reasoning that would be great. Think fashion show, in the now, look at us, we're GLOW Watches. That would be great. Then, I'd like you to speak with Lillian, the leasing agent, and find out when my lease is up. I've lived in this mad apartment building so long I can't remember when Ed and I signed. And with all that's happened with Ed and Mrs. Thornwhistle and Mary Chris, I just can't picture myself spending another happy moment in this place." She looked like she was on the verge of tears and she bit her lip. And I noticed the mauve color she was wearing was perfect for her complexion.

"I'm so sorry you feel that way," I said. The portfolio of watches looked daunting. And it was something I didn't know a thing about.

"Well, how else am I supposed to feel?" she shot back.

"I'll get the leasing information for you as soon as I can."

"Watches first, *please*," she said.

I flipped open the portfolio, "Watches first."

There were so many different styles of watches and collections to choose from—more than I ever knew existed. I had a keen eye for style and fashion, and a task like this was right up my alley. If I could picture one of these watches being promoted on large advertisements at a fashion show, which would it be?

I settled on a watch from the Perfect Timing collection that had yellow gold, everose gold and diamonds around the face. Maybe if I impressed Anita with my fashion sense I could get a job at GLOW.

I took the portfolio over to where Anita was sitting, drinking coffee at the coffee station. Every time someone drank coffee now, I was worried it was poisoned. "I know you're unfocused now," I said.

"And I need to make this decision today. It's like everything in my life decided to fall apart at once."

"I'd go with the yellow and everose gold watch from the Perfect Timing collection," I said. "Because high fashion can never have enough gold."

There was a long pause before she said, "I like it, Cassie. This is it. I will tell the director of fashion shows that the watch was been selected. Now, can you ask about the lease?"

"Right," I said, thinking Anita seemed very focused considering her husband had just been arrested for murder. "The lease."

I found Lillian in the leasing office and asked her quickly to look up Anita's information.

She had the results faster than I thought she would. "Her lease is up in August. We need one month's notice if she's not going to renew."

"Got it," I said. August. That was one month before the fashion show.

When I told Anita the news, she said, "Well, I can tell you right now, I won't be renewing my lease. Not after all that's happened. But there is a lot about the Parkstone I'm going to miss. The sauna for starters."

"I understand," I said. Just then I heard the noise of the fax machine. Royce had written back. I ran over to the concierge desk and got the letter from Royce:

Cassie,

What good news that the murderer has been caught! I cannot tell you how relieved I am that a person capable of such inhumane actions is behind bars. If there is anything I can do to make life at the Parkstone better in these next couple of weeks, please let me know. I thank you for your hard work during this time.

In regards to your wedding venue suggestion, I say, "Congrats!" We'd love to host your wedding at the Parkstone. Once you know a date, pencil it into the calendar, and we'll make the necessary plans. Good news at the Parkstone is always welcomed.

Royce

Wonderful! I couldn't wait to tell Eric the good news. Things at the Parkstone were always a mix of melancholy and joy. Just then, I heard Anita's voice."

CHAPTER 26

The next morning, the lobby was bustling. Every resident wanted to know what had happened yesterday with Ed, and they were happy once I explained Mrs. Thornwhistle's murderer had been caught. Then they wanted to know how Anita was holding up. I understood her desire to move and get away from all these questions.

Mr. Rhodes walked through the lobby for his morning walk with Moola. He gasped when he heard the news. "Don't tell me," he said. "Ed Halpern? Anita's husband? I don't buy it."

"But the detectives took him away," I said. "Anita had been covering for him. She gave him an alibi, but then decided that she wasn't going to cover for him anymore."

"Well, I don't know, he just doesn't really seem like the type," he said.

"To commit murder?" I said.

He gasped and covered Moola's ears. "*Please*," he said. "Keep in mind that dogs have great hearing."

"He lied about his alibi. Mrs. Thornwhistle had caught him cheating, which is motive," I said. "And he had opportunity. He wasn't with Anita that morning."

"Who am I to argue with the law?" he said. "Just saying that I thought he seemed like a reasonable fellow."

I thought about it and said, "Me, too. But all the pieces fit."

Mr. Rhodes and Moola went on their way, and I fielded more questions from residents. The person who seemed the most shocked was Harold Eager. I broke the news to him slowly so he wouldn't have any sudden reactions. I was worried because he was so fragile and I hated for him to hear any more about what had happened to Mrs. Thornwhistle. "The detectives have found someone they believe to be the suspect in Mrs. Thornwhistle's case," I said. "It was resident Ed Halpern."

"Ed?! Whose wife Anita I've talked with frequently?" he said. "Well, why? I want to know why."

I told him about the possible motives and he concluded they must have gotten the right suspect.

"And Stella," he said. "Poor Stella just wanted to watch birds and knit and enjoy life."

"I'm very sorry again for your loss," I said.

"I'm grateful they caught the person," he said. "Imagine if we never knew who was responsible. I think that would be too much for me to handle."

I nodded. "I'm glad everything has resolved."

"Now," he continued, "I was just in the library and it crossed my mind. Tell me if you think this would be a crazy idea, but I was thinking that you and Royce have been so nice to let me stay here in one of the guest rooms...I was thinking, wouldn't it be grand to live here?"

"I think that's a wonderful idea, Mr. Eager," I said. "I think Mrs. Thornwhistle would approve, too."

"I can help carry on her legacy," he said. "And, well, the lovebirds are already here, so I can take them off your hands. What do you think?"

"I say why wait?"

"Cassie, you are a wonderful concierge. I just can't wait to honor Stella and live at the Parkstone."

∞

Later that night, as I was filling out my application to the Fashion College, Eric called.

"Hey," he said, "do you have a minute?"

I stopped typing. "Any excuse to not work on my application," I said. "Plus, it's you."

"Cassie," he said, "I can't wrap my head around something."

"What's going on?" I said.

"It's just that, yes, Ed had motive and he doesn't have an alibi, but we just don't have enough evidence linking him."

"Their wasn't much evidence at the scene of the crime," I said.

"You mentioned the earrings," he said. "Ed seemed to know nothing about those. Do you remember anything else that you saw that could be suspicious?"

I squinted my eyes and tried to remember the crime scene. "There was a gum wrapper," I said finally. "I remember a crinkled-up gum wrapper next to the body."

"Is there any resident you know of who chews gum that we can place at the scene of the crime?"

"Not that I know of," I said. "It's not ringing a bell." All of a sudden my head hurt. Did we not get the right person? I had told all the residents and Royce that we'd caught the culprit. Harold was so happy he was even moving into the building. "Eric, please tell me we didn't mess up."

"I just need more to convict him," he said. "And I was hoping you could help me find it."

Now, filling out my application seemed a lot less stressful. "I'll do the best I can," I said, "but I've told you everything I know." Then I thought about it some more. "Actually, I do remember noticing some teal-colored sequins on the oriental rug near Mrs. Thornwhistle's body."

"What were they from?" he said.

I grimaced. "That's anybody's guess. But they did seem really out of place."

"So someone wearing a garment with sequins could have been at the crime scene," he said.

"Or someone chewing gum," I said. "Didn't your guys collect these items as evidence?"

"I'm sure it's in the evidence room, but I just wanted your recollection of what seemed out of place right after the murder."

"So, a tackily-dressed gum chewer is what we're looking for."

"Cassie, this is not a joke," he said.

"I know, it's just that I still think we got the right guy," I said. "And everything at the Parkstone has gone back to normal, so I don't want to rock that boat."

"Will you call me if you remember anything else?" he said.

"You'll be the first person I call," I said.

Now I had to get back to my application, if I wanted to become a personal shopper and ever move beyond the craziness of the Parkstone.

CHAPTER 27

The next morning, the fashionable Mrs. Canterbury stopped by the concierge desk bright and early. "What do you say to almond raspberry chocolate croissants from the devilishly good bakery down the street?" she said, placing a large bag of pastries on the desk. Then she adjusted the collar of her gold quilted jacket that I'd picked out for her. Along with the straight leg white jeans, and the red and white striped Kate Spade flats. I was already practically Mrs. Canterbury's personal shopper, but I'd need the certificate from Fashion College if I wanted to make strides in the industry.

"I say, 'Why of course! I'd love one,'" I said, as she placed a dainty croissant on a plate. "And what about your detective friend? Will he be stopping by today?"

I thought if Eric stopped by it would only be to impart bad news, so I was hoping not. "I don't know," I said. "He's really busy with the case."

"Oh yes, the case!" she said. "Is Ed Halpern really the—dare I say—murderer?"

"As far as we know, yes," I said, biting into the delicious chocolate croissant. "But it's not a closed case just yet."

"You and the detectives worked so quickly this time," she said. "If anything should ever happen to me, I'd want you to investigate it."

"Well, thanks, Mrs. Canterbury," I said. "But please don't think like that. Everything at the Parkstone is back to normal now."

"As long as we always have our trusty concierge, we'll be fine," Mrs. Canterbury said.

I didn't want to worry Mrs. Canterbury, but I was so excited about the possibility of getting my online personal shopping certificate. "Well, I love being the Parkstone's daytime concierge," I said. "I'm also applying to a personal shopping certificate program at the Fashion College."

She clapped her hands. "Why, that's wonderful! You have such an eye for detail."

I smiled. "And I was hoping you'd write me a recommendation."

"Why, I'd love to," she said, showing off her jacket and the rest of her outfit. "I don't look this fashionable just by chance."

"Thank you," I said. "I love being a concierge at the Parkstone, but I'd love to be in the fashion industry as well."

"You got it," she said. "I'll write it out on paper, and then if you want, you can type it up or whatever works for you."

Mrs. Canterbury was the best. She continued, "I'm going to head upstairs now. I guess it's a good thing we didn't see your detective friend." She placed another croissant on the plate. "Just in case he shows up. This is the Parkstone after all."

Then I remembered to tell Mrs. Canterbury about the venue update for my wedding.

"Wonderful!" she said. "When do I get an invitation?"

There was still a date to set. But we were getting there.

Mrs. Canterbury walked to the elevators, just as Mrs. Olive walked into the lobby through the revolving doors. She was the only resident I could remember who'd ever talked about taking sleeping medicine.

"How is it out there, Mrs. Olive?" I said.

"Still a bit chilly," she said. "You'd think we're still waiting for spring."

Mrs. Olive was plump and had an engaging Midwestern accent. She had an issue of the *Bethesda Monthly* tucked between her arm and her purse. I thought of Mrs. Thornwhistle's smiling face inside.

"Did you see Mrs. Thornwhistle in the story about the knitting competition?"

"Oh, I haven't read it yet," she said. "Just picked it up at the Just Sew boutique down the street."

"So you sew?" I said.

"My whole life," she said. "I sewed this quilted purse." She struck a pose showcasing her tan-colored quilted purse. It was beautiful. Between her purse and Mrs. Canterbury's jacket, it looked like the quilted look was in. She continued, "Mrs. Thornwhistle was a knitter. I knew that because she thought she was better than everyone else, especially me because I sew instead of knit."

"So, there was friction between you two?"

"Enough to cause a raging fire," she said.

"I'm sorry to hear that," I said.

"Don't be. I'm sorry to hear she's dead, but I can't say I ever got along with her," she said.

"Are you still having trouble sleeping?" I said.

"That was months ago," she said. "Haven't had trouble since the doctor prescribed me that new sleeping medicine."

My face lit up. This could be the evidence we needed. She continued, "Why do you look so happy? A second ago we were just talking about how I was sleeping like a bat."

"Excuse me," I said. "In all seriousness. Sleeping medicine was what the detectives discovered killed Mrs. Thornwhistle."

She gasped. "I thought it was peanuts!"

"They were wrong. It was sleeping medicine," I said.

Just then Mrs. Olive reached into her purse and brought out a carefully wrapped piece of gum. She plopped it in her mouth and crinkled the wrapper, putting it back in her purse.

It looked just like the crinkled wrapper found at the crime scene. Mrs. Olive, who always seemed so cheery, was now seeming very sinister to me.

"Why are you giving me such an evil stare?" she asked. "Cassie, one minute you're happy as a button, the next you look like you've seen a ghost."

"There was a crinkled gum wrapper left at the scene of the crime," I said.

"And you think I did it?" she said, bopping me over the head with the rolled up magazine. "You're full of nonsense. You're a great concierge, but leave the sleuthing up to that hunky detective fiancé of yours."

Then I mustered all the courage I had. "Were you in the club room the morning of Mrs. Thornwhistle's death?"

"Why of course I was," she said. "Just like everybody else. I dropped off a dessert for her birthday party. I brought the lemon custard pie."

"I'm sorry, Mrs. Olive," I said. "We've just all been on edge. I think for the sake of keeping my sanity, I'll just have to assume the murderer has been caught. And the case has been solved." There was so much else I had to concentrate on: my Fashion College application, being there for the residents, and planning a wedding.

"Well, this murder has all of us crazy," she said.

"Did you see Mrs. Thornwhistle the morning of her birthday?"

"No, doll," she said. "I just dropped off the dessert, which I confess ended up being a little too tart."

Mrs. Olive's biggest worry was that the pie she brought was too tart. I really needed to get a handle on things. Life wasn't as bleak as it seemed when I thought about was the case. A break from the case was exactly what I needed.

Just then, Eric and a couple of other detectives walked through the revolving doors. I'd spoken too soon.

They walked with determination. "Good day," Eric said to Mrs. Olive, who batted her eyes. Then I handed him the plate with the croissant. "Courtesy of Mrs. Canterbury," I said. He smiled. "And just in time for breakfast." He looked at the other detectives. "Great timing, guys." Then his smile turned serious and he said, "Cassie, we're here to talk with Anita Halpern."

Anita? What could they want with the fashion executive? "About what?" I said.

"You'll see," he said. Just then, Anita walked through the lobby as Mr. Rhodes walked through the revolving door with Moola. There was always a lot happening at once at the Parkstone. Anita looked very chic with the collar of her black trench coat turned up, and her large gold jewelry and GLOW watch in stark contrast.

"Mrs. Halpern," Eric said, "you're just who we want to see."

Then Mr. Rhodes stood next to me with Moola at his side. "Cassie, what's going on here?"

"I don't know yet," I said. "We'll find out."

Then Anita took off her sunglasses and said to Eric, "If it's about Ed, I don't have anything more to say. I've said all I know."

"Good guess," he said. "It's about Ed. But we're not asking for a comment."

Mr. Rhodes picked up Moola and turned to me. "This is getting good."

"There's never a dull moment," I said.

Then detective Williams spoke up. "We don't have enough evidence to keep Ed," he said. "So, he will be set free this afternoon."

"What?" Anita said, yelling. "You're kidding me. He's coming *back*? You let him out? But he killed Mrs. Thornwhistle."

"That's just it," Eric spoke up again. "We don't have enough proof. He won't be back right away, but we won't be able to keep him forever."

Something told me Anita's move-out date had just gotten pushed up.

CHAPTER 28

Mr. Eager walked through the lobby from the library. "There are some great books in that library," he said. "Even some history books about the war. Brought me back some years thinking about it and about how Stella and I would read together in a small reading nook in our living room before I left. There were moments when everything was perfect. Sometimes it takes many years to realize that."

"I'm glad you're enjoying the Parkstone amenities," I said. "You can enjoy them everyday when you move here."

"I have an appointment with Lillian about my lease in fifteen minutes," he said. "I'll just hang out around the lobby until it's time. I'd make myself a coffee, but now every time I think of coffee, I think of Stella. I just can't bring myself to drink any." He paused. "Do you remember anything else from the morning she was killed, Cassie?"

Now Harold was becoming a sleuth like me! "What I remember I've already told Eric," I said. I truly believed the culprit had knocked on Mrs. Thornwhistle's apartment door and since Mrs. Thornwhistle knew who it was she let them in. What excuse would someone have? What would they have to talk about? I thought about the *Bethesda Monthly* that I'd seen on her kitchen counter, and how excited Mrs. Thornwhistle must have been to be featured as a competition winner. Someone could have dropped off the copy and stayed to talk about it with ample opportunity to poison her coffee. That was it, I was sure of it!

"Eric seems like a very amiable young man. Sounds like you've got yourself a great companion. Don't do what I did and go and ruin it," he said.

"I won't," I said. My relationship with Eric was the only thing I could count on among all the craziness.

"Are you sure there's not more you know, Cassie," he said. "You know, it's just a fluke that I stopped by the Parkstone at all. I had mailed the lovebirds assuming they'd arrive at the correct destination. When I didn't hear back from Stella I assumed it was because she didn't want to talk to me. Now, I'll never know."

"I wish I had more to tell you, Harold," I said. Behind the concierge desk, I found a box of the guest truffles. "Since you've been such a delightful guest. And to show our gratitude that you've decided to rent at the Parkstone."

"I don't usually eat sweets, but I can make an exception," he said.

Just then, Lillian stepped out from the leasing office. "Harold Eager?" she said. "Are you ready to talk about your lease?"

"Fire away!" he said.

"I think you're just going to love living at the Parkstone," she said as Harold stepped into her office. "Don't you think?"

CHAPTER 29

A couple days later, after Harold had signed a lease with a September move-in date, he gathered his belongings, as well as the lovebirds and moved out of the guest room. It was a sad day. Harold had been a staple of the Parkstone for more than a week, and he was going to be missed. I was going to miss the feathery duo, too, who had learned more phrases I'd taught them like, "I love the Parkstone."

"I'll be back soon, Cassie," Harold said. "At least now Parkstonians don't think I'm a ghost haunting the place as Stella had suggested."

"Yes, that's good to know," I said. "Will you make it home okay?"

"I'm just across the Potomac in Virginia," he said. "I'm not leaving for the war again."

"Well, we'll see you in September," I said.

"And hopefully, the murder will be solved for good by then?" he said, standing there carrying his duffle bag in one hand and the bird cage in the other.

"Eric and the other detectives are doing everything they can," I said. And I just wished there was more I could remember to help move the case along.

"See you in September," he said. "Now let's go Peachy and Keen."

"Let's go, Let's go. I love the Parkstone!" they said back.

Eventually, over time, life got back to normal at the Parkstone. It was quiet without the lovebirds around repeating every phrase, but Jet-Setter and Cashmere kept it lively enough. I was able to focus enough and submit my application for Fashion College, with a very favorable letter of recommendation from Mrs. Canterbury. Eric would stop in every so often to check on me and see how everything was going. But there was nothing to report. Anita and Ed had each moved out on separate occasions, leaving their apartment vacant and available for a new Parkstonian to move in.

About a month later, there was a service held for Stella which many of the Parkstonians, and Harold, attended, followed by a reception in the lobby organized by a few of the Parkstonians who were closest to her. The reception was catered by the Parkstone, too, and there were delicious smoked salmon filets, with olive oil and vinegar on top of asparagus. Hot, fresh out of the oven, dinner rolls, were accompanied by a side dish of roasted garlic and dill potatoes and a mango avocado salsa. Then there were the desserts: Large layered chocolate and raspberry mousse cakes, along with raspberry tarts, and chocolate tarts with strawberries and pistachios. I had a slice of the layered cake, which was just the right texture. It was delicious. How I had wished Mrs. Thornwhistle was there with us.

Mrs. Canterbury was one of the residents who helped organize the event. She was dressed in a black sheath dress, I'd helped her pick it out and paired it with a black cardigan and bright coral red lipstick. "I think that it was necessary to have the reception at the Parkstone," she said, shuddering. "What a tragedy."

Then I shuddered. "I hate to think the murderer is still out there."

Then Mr. Rhodes, wearing a black suit and bow tie, walked through the crowd with Moola, who was wearing a black knit sweater. He approached us as we all shared our condolences. "I hope they find whoever did this, is all I'm saying," he said. "I don't know how long Moola and I can go on knowing we're living amongst a murderer."

"I agree," I said. "This is the longest a case has gone unsolved at the Parkstone."

Mr. Rhodes gasped. "How many cases have there been?"

I wished I hadn't brought it up. "Not many," I said.

"Which is how many?" he said.

"There have been three," I said. "But the other two were solved, not lingering over our heads like this."

"Well, what about you, Cassie?" Mr. Rhodes said. "Where were you the morning she was killed?"

Mrs. Canterbury gasped. "How dare you!" she said. "Cassie works very hard as the Parkstone concierge, and she does a great job. Imagine keeping control of this insane place."

But Mr. Rhodes continued, "It just crossed my mind that you were the only one not questioned. Very convenient that your fiancé is lead detective on the case. Who needs an alibi when you have an in with the detective force?"

"Mr. Rhodes, I know this reception is a stressful, somber time, but there's no need for you to lash out at me," I said. "I spoke with Mrs. Thornwhistle briefly as she was preparing for her birthday party, but I went nowhere near her coffee mug. And I have no motive."

He looked as though he was thinking about this. "True," he said. "You wouldn't have a motive." He threw his hands up in the air. "No one would. Mrs. Thornwhistle was a great human being."

I nodded. That was the problem. Maybe motive was what we should focus on. Once we discovered the motive, then we'd find the murderer.

"Look, Cassie," Mr. Rhodes said. "I'm sorry I lashed out at you; it's just all so unnerving."

"That's okay," I said. "I just hope people can move on, and get some closure after tonight."

Mrs. Canterbury threw her hands up in the air. "Well, we don't have a choice now do we?"

CHAPTER 30

After I helped get the caterers packed up and organized, I went to the mailboxes to check my mail. There was a stack of mail, most of it junk, but I managed to salvage the important letters. There was a letter from the Fashion College that they had received my application. They would be making their decision before the start of the school year. I tucked away the letter to keep it safe. I had a good feeling about my application.

Next, there was a letter from my mom. She wrote that the family was great, and that I should get better about answering my phone. Also, had Eric and I picked a date? That was a good nudge in the right direction. Then there was the latest edition of *Glamour* magazine. Yes, my favorite. I hugged the magazine close. There was already an article I wanted to read on the cover about great finds at second hand stores.

Then there was one more letter to go through. I didn't recognize the New York address. Who could it be from? I opened the letter and to my surprise it was from the editors of *Runway Magazine* about fashion week. The words *Contest Winner* graced the front of the letter. *You have won a chance to attend New York's fashion week in September.* I couldn't believe it. I was going to fashion week. I gathered all the mail I was keeping and dumped the rest. I closed my mailbox. I needed to hurry back to my apartment. I'd need to share this good news with someone.

CHAPTER 31

"What's up?" Eric said on the other line.

"I didn't tell you this," I said, "because it was a long shot, and I wasn't sure I was going to win, but I won a contest to attend a fashion show in September in New York during fashion week."

"That's great!" he said. "I'm so happy for you. That's, that's just so, perfect for you."

"I think so," I said. "So I'm going to respond to the letter saying I'll be there. I mean, of course, I'll be there, it's fashion week. All of the big shots, anyone who has anything to do with fashion will *be* there."

"Great," he said. "So I take it you're going."

"You bet," I said. "I haven't taken a vacation from the Parkstone since I started my concierge job, but I don't think the place will fall apart without me."

"That's saying a lot, Cassie," he said. "But I don't think it should stop you from going."

"Right," I said. "I'm going. And my next question is, will you go with me?"

"To fashion week?" he said. "I don't know. It's not really my thing."

"Not the fashion show, but go with me to New York. We can take the Acela train together. It will be fun."

There was a long pause. "When is this again?"

"The first week of September," I said.

Another long pause. "I guess I could work something out. There's a precinct in New York where I have some friends I could meet up with."

"Perfect," I said. "We'll take the train from Bethesda and stay a couple of days in New York. I'll be busy with fashion distractions and you can visit your detective friends."

"You got it," he said. "By the way, how did everything go with Mrs. Thornwhistle's reception tonight?"

"It went as to be expected," I said. "It was such a somber occasion, and there was also a lot of anger. Even residents lashing out at me as if I could have done it. Can you imagine?"

"You did find the body," Eric said. "So I understand it's a natural assumption. But completely invalid. We're looking for someone who's a cold-blooded killer. And someone who has motive. We're just not able to figure out who that is."

"Well, if the murder still isn't solved in September, which I hope it is, the fashion show will be a nice respite from the case."

Just then, I remembered that I'd also helped choose the yellow and everose gold watch to be featured on GLOW Watches advertisements during fashion week. Eric talked more about the case, but my mind was elsewhere. It was settled. In September, we'd be in New York.

CHAPTER 32

The Acela train was comfortable. Eric and I had a sleeper car that had enough room for us to stretch out. I sat near the window reading *Glamour* magazine's nail polish colors for spring. It was the first time I'd been away from the Parkstone on a vacation, and I tried to distract my mind from all the things at the Parkstone that could go wrong.

Eric had just gone to the dining car to get us breakfast and drinks.

I loved the sounds of the train, the monotony of the wheels on the tracks and the clanging of the open doors and the whistle. The train ride was only three hours and twenty-five minutes, and we were already halfway there. There was only a short amount of time standing between me and the world of fashion. I looked in the mirror. I was dressed for the occasion. I had styled my hair so that my bangs were sleek along my forehead and top of my nose. And I'd curled my long dark brown tresses with a curling iron. I was wearing an off-the-shoulder navy blue crepe sheath dress with whimsical bell sleeves. I felt amazing, and couldn't wait to see the fashion collections and eye-catching runway outfits at the show.

Moments later, Eric returned with a tray with two plates of pancakes, and two glasses of orange juice.

"I think I'm going to have a Sprite," I said, craving the soft drink.

"Alright," he said. "I'll be right back."

"Don't worry," I said. "I'll get it." This way I'd have a chance to explore the train, too. I walked down the corridors of the train, a part of me was pretending *I* was on a fashion runway. I was letting my shoulders fall back, keeping my head up high, taking long strides just when someone else, carrying a perforated luggage bag swung around the corner. I lost my balance in my new high heels and fell to the ground.

"Cassie!" the voice said. "I almost didn't recognize you; you're so dressed up."

I looked up to see Mr. Rhodes standing above me holding my arm to help me up.

"Mr. Rhodes, what are you doing here?" I said, confused at seeing him outside of the Parkstone.

He smiled. "I'm going to fashion week. What about you? You're not at the Parkstone. I just always expect you're going to be there."

I smiled. "I'm going to fashion week as well."

Mrs. Rhodes opened the zipper of the perforated pet carrier bag he was holding. "Me and Moola just can't wait to see the Bell fashion dresses on the runway. I do their marketing."

He then brought Moola out of the carrier. She was wearing a teal knit sweater with teal-colored sequins. My jaw dropped.

"Cassie, are you feeling okay? One minute you're falling on the floor, the next you're mesmerized like in a far-off world," he said.

"Teal sequins," I repeated under my breath.

"Aren't they great? They're Moola's favorite color," he said, moving her paw to wave.

I braced myself between the walls of the train's rocky corridor and said, "They're the color of the sequins that were found on the carpet in the club room, the morning Mrs. Thornwhistle was murdered." Fright set in. Why did I say that? I could be on the train with a killer.

Mr. Rhodes took a step back. Then another step, as he began to run back toward the dining hall. Just then, the sleeper car door at the end of the hall opened and Eric stepped out. "Cassie, is everything okay?"

"Follow me," I said, walking as quickly as I could down the corridor to catch up with Mr. Rhodes. His back was turned toward me and he was walking as fast as he could with Moola's bag carrier tucked under his arm. He opened the door to the dining car and shut it with full force. I lifted up the ends of my dress so I wouldn't trip in my heels, or worse yet, rip the dress.

Eric was right behind me now. "Cassie, what's going on?"

"It's Mr. Rhodes, from the Parkstone," I said. "I think he's guilty."

"Of what?" he said, as we reached the dining car.

"Killing Mrs. Thornwhistle," I said. "Let's go." I told Eric about the sequins, which he remembered from the police report. Finally, he said, "I guess we can talk with him, but I think it's a longshot."

Eric and I walked briskly through the dining car. There was no sight of Mr. Rhodes. My heels were beginning to hurt in my new shoes and my morale was low. But we searched each car of the train until we'd determined that Mr. Rhodes and the pooch had outsmarted us.

"I know you're demoralized, Cassie," he said, "but as I remember, Mr. Rhodes had an airtight alibi?"

"What was it?" I said as we took a seat in two empty seats in the last train, and my feet felt relieved that my heels were finally off.

"He was at a doggie day care for Moola," he said. "And we asked his instructor. His alibi checked out."

"But the teal sequins place him at the crime scene," I said. "That's something."

"But it doesn't guarantee guilt," Eric said. "Come on, let's go."

Eric helped me up as I threw my body over his as and he carried me through six train cars and a dining car to ours. We had just settled in for the last fifteen minutes of the train ride when there was a knock on our sleeper car's door.

"Who is it?" Eric said sternly.

"Mr. Rhodes." There was a pause. "And Moola."

I could feel my eyes almost pop out of my head. "He found us?"

"I think he's innocent. Why else would he be coming to us," Eric said to me before opening the door. "What can we help you with Mr. Rhodes."

Mr. Rhodes dodged around Eric and said, "Hi, Cassie." Then with more seriousness he said, "Detective Peters." Eric nodded. Mr. Rhodes looked sheepish. "I'm sorry for running earlier. Cassie, you just had this look in your eye like you were going to catch the killer. And I'm here to assure you I am *not* him."

People could say anything. "Did you see Mrs. Thornwhistle that morning?"

"Briefly," he said standing in the doorway or our cramped sleeper car, "I'll tell you what happened. I didn't even want to bring anything or attend her birthday bash, but my wife Penelope thought it would be a good idea to make amends. So, I brought strawberry cupcakes that I'd bought at a Bethesda bakery and was leaving them on the table. I had Moola under one arm, and she was making such a fuss with all the desserts that I put Moola down on the oriental rug. That's when the sequins must have fallen off."

I wanted more information. "But you ran into Mrs. Thornwhistle?"

"Unfortunately. She was grateful for the birthday wishes, but glad Moola and I were going to be at a doggie daycare class and unable to attend her party. Anyway, sorry to break the good and bad news. Thought it was better than you chasing me around the train as if I were the culprit."

I felt somewhat embarrassed that I'd taken off with full force in heels down the train's corridor in a mad hunt for what I thought was Mrs. Thornwhistle's killer. I nodded in defeat and looked up at Eric. "Back to square one," I said.

I looked around the cabin. Our uneaten stacks of pancakes and orange juice. I had forgotten to get my Sprite.

All of this chaos and I hadn't even gotten to fashion week yet.

CHAPTER 33

After the train arrived in Penn Station and we said goodbye to Mr. Rhodes and Moola, Eric went to the precinct to spend time with his detective friends he hadn't seen in years. I told him to mention the case of Mrs. Thornwhistle and see if any of them had any new angles to the case we hadn't yet considered. He agreed begrudgingly.

I took the subway to the West Village and after I'd followed the map a bit, I made it to the Industria location for fashion week. I knew I was close because I could hear the techno music from a block away as I walked confidently with my NYFW contest badge. I wished Eric or my mom were here to see this, but I also realized they'd both be happy with just a selfie of me from the event. I snapped a picture of myself in front of a poster of some Yves Saint Laurent models with dry ice emerging from the sides. Perfect!

Then I waited in line and when it was my turn, I handed my contest-winning NYFW badge over to the door attendant. My palms were sweaty. The attendant scanned my badge and said, "Great seat. You'll be in the fourth row."

"The fourth row?!"

"Yes," he said. "Now if you don't mind. There are a lot of people in line."

"Of course," I said, moving right through. Inside, it was complete chaos. There were tall, thin models walking around swiftly in high sleek heels. Some of them had rollers in their hair, others looked like they had been through the hair and makeup process already and were sporting natural looks, bouffants which reminded me of Anita, and cascading curls.

I was happy with the navy blue off the shoulder dress I had chosen to wear, but thought maybe I could have paid more attention to my gloss and mascara. Also, my hair was losing its curl.

Trendy people rolled dollies full of expensive, couture clothes past me in every direction. I was almost going in circles. I was totally caught up in all of it.

Then, when I looked up, I noticed the GLOW Watch advertisement which I'd helped Anita choose. There was the yellow and everose gold watch with diamonds, with the caption: *In Time for Fashion.* It looked great!

Of all my life experiences, this so far was the top. It was on par with how it felt to nab a bad guy. I continued past all the clothes to an open door. I walked in. There were bright lights and lots of commotion. I found a seat and plopped down in a twirly chair facing a large row of mirrors. I just needed to catch my breath. I pulled my brochure with a map from my purse to find out where I was going. In the process, I found an index card that I'd put together from an article I'd read in *In Style* magazine that helped with the pronunciation of some of the designers' names. I was practicing aloud the name *Givenchy* (zhee-vawn-SHEE) when all of a sudden, a hairstylist approach wielding a curling iron.

"Givenchy?" he said with authority. "They're going with the lovely cascading curls, lots of hairspray, and bounce."

"Oh, I'm not one of..." I started to say. I was going to tell him I wasn't one of the models. But then I figured if I was at fashion week, I might as well indulge. He began wrapping my hair around the curling iron. Then came the hairspray. Then, with my best accent possible, I said, "Givenchy!"

CHAPTER 34

The hairstylist was amazing! My hair looked like I belonged in a hair commercial. I slid off the chair and thanked him profusely, but he was on to a real model. *Wait until Eric hears this*, I thought. I wandered out of the dressing rooms, and made my way to the backstage area. There were so many people, and they all looked so fancy, wearing edgy glasses, fancy suits, perfectly pointy dress shoes, ruffles, satin, and velvet. I was trying to pinpoint what was in style for the season, but there seemed to be so many different looks.

Finally, I wandered around through a curtain and found the stage area and my fourth row seat. I was so close to the front I could see Anna Wintour right in front of me. The lights flickered, and the techno music began to blare. People began to settle into their seats. This was the ten-minute warning that the show was about to begin. The first collection down the runway would be Prada's—their name displayed at the foot of the long runway. Then lights began to light up the runway.

In my seat, I was people watching those around me and across the way. I looked across the runway and saw a woman with a bouffant hairstyle and a khaki jacket, with the collar popped up, a black and white striped blouse with red high-waisted crepe pants. I'd recognize that bouffant hairstyle anywhere. It was Anita Halpern, GLOW's hair and makeup executive and now ex-wife of Ed Halpern. I waved but she didn't see me. I got an idea. I'd surprise her. She would be thrilled to know I was at the fashion show, I was sure.

I left my dark denim jean jacket on my chair and took the long way around the runway. As I approached the second row, the group around Anita began to disperse.

"Anita!" I said as she turned around.

"Cassie?" she said. "What are you doing at fashion week? Your hair looks great."

I was going to tell her how they had mistakenly thought I was one of the models, but I stopped short. My good disposition had all of a sudden turned to dread.

Chills shook my body as I realized a dark truth: Ed Halpern hadn't murdered Mrs. Thornwhistle as I had thought all this time. Anita must have set him up. The tell-tale clue—even though she averted her gaze as she stood right in front of me—were the unmistakable pineapple-shaped carved jade and gold clip-on earrings visible above her jacket collar.

I began to feel as if I didn't want to be at fashion week. I wanted to be back at the Parkstone with Jet-Setter and Cashmere and Eric. Eric! I'd have to call Eric and let him know. Now, I was sure of the killer.

With every bit of restraint I could muster, I asked Anita to excuse me. I had a phone call to make.

Once she was turned, talking to someone else, I picked up my phone and called my detective fiancé. "Eric," I said, "I need to talk to you."

"I hope you're having fun. The selfie looked great. Sounds loud there," he said.

"I know who the killer is," I said, talking as quietly as I could. "She moved out, but she was right in front of our noses all this time—Anita Halpern."

"Cassie, you're at fashion week," he said. "You're supposed to be enjoying yourself."

"I can't," I said. "Not now. Not knowing that Mrs. Thornwhistle's killer is in the second row at New York fashion week."

"What makes you suspect Mrs. Halpern?"

"She's wearing the earrings," I said. "The ones Mrs. Thornwhistle was wearing the day she was killed and then went missing."

"And Ed couldn't have given them to her?" he said.

"I don't think Ed's that careless," I said. "And I think Anita is so brazen she thinks she'll never get caught."

"Cassie, do not chase her," Eric said. "I'll be right there."

"Second row!" I shouted.

There were now two minutes before the show was scheduled to begin. Why had Anita worn the earrings? Surely she realized they were a major clue to her guilt. I figured that it just showed that Anita couldn't help herself. What was her original motive anyway? I had to know.

I walked back to Anita. "I couldn't help but notice *your* earrings?"

"Of course, they're my earrings, Cassie. I got them from a second-hand shop in the upper east side."

Then all my anger from the unsolved case just spewed out. Those were the pineapple-shaped carved jade gold and diamond earrings that Harold Eager, who now lived in the Parkstone, from home from the war for his love Stella Thornwhistle.

"Those are not from a second-hand shop," I said.

She looked startled. I continued, "So my second question is why? Why did you kill Mrs. Thornwhistle?" The music was blaring and I was shouting at the top of my lungs at this point. I was standing next to a very stylish heavyset man who was wearing a white button down shirt and bright red suspenders with sharp navy slacks. On Anita's right was an older couple, the woman wearing an extravagant black hat that defied gravity with had a bird on top.

"Cassie, you're out of your mind. I think all that makeup and curling went to your head."

"You can deny it to me," I said, "but when Detective Peters gets here, he'll demand answers."

Just then, Anita took off in her high heels. I could feel the curls on my shoulders bouncing to great heights as I followed after her. Just then, the lights stopped their frantic pace and the music tempo got quicker. The show was about to begin. Models started to walk down the runway just as Anita crossed over it with me following right after her.

It was a mess! Models fell and yelled on the runway, as Anita inadvertently thwarted their path. I slid as quickly as I could across as a model somersaulted over me and yelled, "My Prada high heels!" The next one dove on top of the first one. Anita and I had caused a model pile up.

Once across the runway, I followed Anita as she ran into a dressing room. She pushed dollies full of couture clothing in my way. And I pushed them away as quickly as I could. Then it was silent. Where had she gone?

Then, out of the corner of my eye, I saw her crouched under a mirror and behind a director-style chair. There was a stand with some Coach's fluffy, feathery boas next to me. I grabbed a bright yellow one and lunged toward where Anita was hiding. Grabbing her arms, I used the boa to tie her to a banister near the dressing room tables.

"Eric will be here soon," I said. "You're not going anywhere with those earrings."

"Cassie," she said, "if only you'd just stick to being a concierge."

CHAPTER 35

Eric arrived on the scene a few minutes later. "Phew," I said. "I wasn't sure how long I was going to be able to keep her like this."

"A brightly colored boa?" Eric said. "Really, Cassie? Perfect way to catch a high-fashion killer."

Anita tried to writhe out of the boa constraint. "I am not a killer," she said.

"How do you explain the earrings?" I said. "I know those are Mrs. Thornwhistle's. They're unmistakable."

"Fine," she said. "I'm a respectable person. And so was Ed, until he met that Mary Chris Farley. And then Mrs. Thornwhistle and to get in on it. She just *had* to be looking out the courtyard window. She just had to put her big nose where it didn't belong. Kind of like you, Cassie." She paused. "But I have too much style for that. So I decided if I knocked off Mrs. Thornwhistle, then maybe Ed would settle down. But no, he kept looking at Mary Chris like a puppy dog, so I decided to frame him. It was the perfect crime. Two birds with one stone. Just like those stupid birds you brought into the lobby! I'm sure the police would have been satisfied that Ed killed Mrs. Thornwhistle until you, Cassie, started nosing, and you convinced your fiancé that you didn't have enough evidence to convict Ed."

"Now, we have more than enough to convict you," I said, as Eric handcuffed her. "Now you'll be wearing a different type of stripes."

She growled as the detectives took her away. Eric hugged my shoulders. "That was a close one. I'm glad I got here on time," he said.

"I'm glad I spotted the earrings," I said. Then I looked at one of the security guards who'd been there when I slid across the Prada runway. "Any chance the show will go on?"

He shook his head and grunted.

Eric took my hand. "You know, now might be a good time to leave."

I took one last look at my perfect bouncy curls in the mirror and wrapped a bright blue Coach boa around me and Eric and gave him a kiss.

"Cassie," he said. "This also might be a good time to leave the boa."

I smiled and gave him another kiss. "We caught the killer. Now everything can go back to normal." And at that moment, nothing else mattered.

CHAPTER 36

Eric and I took the three and half hour train ride back to Washington, D.C. that afternoon. I couldn't wait to tell the Parkstonians the good news. The first person I saw when we walked through the lobby's revolving doors with our rolling luggage was Harold. He was drinking a mug of tea and reading the newspaper in the near end of the lobby.

"How was fashion week?" he said, putting down the newspaper.

"The fashion was great, and the murder suspects were even better," I said.

"What?!" said Harold. "Did you find yourself involved in another mystery?"

"Nope," I said, stacking my luggage. "Same one."

Harold looked incredulous. "How on earth?"

Eric stepped forward. "We've made an arrest in the case of Mrs. Thornwhistle." He looked at me. "And it's really because of Cassie that we did."

"Why, Cassie, who was it?" he said.

I explained about Anita and how she'd stolen the earrings that Harold had brought back from Burma. And how we got them back, although they were presently in police custody.

"Anita?" he said. "How wretched. What a wretched thing to do."

"The good news is that things can finally go back to normal," I said. "Have I missed anything at the Parkstone?"

"You weren't even gone a day," Harold said. "You don't leave this place often do you?"

"Well, I definitely left my mark on New York's fashion week," I said, smiling.

Eric put his hand on my shoulder. He smirked. "That's for sure."

I looked at the blue fluffy boa sticking out of my luggage bag. "And Coach's Executive Creative Director even gave me a boa for my work to help the NYPD," I said, knowing that I would wear the boa every chance I got.

Eric smiled. "It was quite an adventure."

"But nothing compares to the Parkstone," I said, breathing in that distinctive marble floor smell.

The next morning, I didn't have to work at the concierge desk. They had hired a temp because I had thought I was still going to be in New York. I had all this time, and didn't know what to do with it. I put on my jeans and wore an embroidered shirt with the bright blue boa. *Why not.* It was still fashion week after all.

I went to the club room and sat on the green velvet cushion in the reading window where Mrs. Thornwhistle used to bird watch. The one where she'd seen Ed and Mary Chris. And maybe where she'd spent hours a day daydreaming.

When I stood up, the velvet cushion was askew. I went to move it and noticed there was a wooden lid under the cushion. I opened the top of the wooden built-in seat. Inside, there were skeins of yarn and knitting needles and a finished knit blue and green striped scarf––the scarf Mrs. Thornwhistle had knit for Mr. Beasley. He thought she had never even started knitting it, and here it was—completely knit—a promise kept.

THE END

ABOUT THE AUTHOR

Sherry Lodge has been writing for more than a decade for both print and online. She's written for local newspapers in both Massachusetts and Washington, D.C., where she currently writes and edits web material for a major non-profit organization.

In addition to writing, Sherry loves to watch golf, which inspired Kip Ace as one of the main characters in the first in her Cassie Hall mystery series—*Courtyard Corpse*. *Club Room Corpse* is the third in this series, following *Cloakroom Corpse*. Sherry has a master's degree in journalism from Boston University.